I0690598

THE INLET

First Edition

Published by The Nazca Plains Corporation
Las Vegas, Nevada
2011

ISBN: 978-1-61098-097-5
Ebook: 978-1-61098-098-2

Published by

The Nazca Plains Corporation ®
4640 Paradise Rd, Suite 141
Las Vegas NV 89109-8000

PUBLISHER'S NOTE
The Inlet is a work of fiction created wholly by *Hank Brooks'* imagination. All characters are fictional and any resemblance to any persons living or deceased is purely by accident. No portion of this book reflects any real person or events.

City Photo, Daniel Korzeniewski
Holding Hands Photo, Purmar

Art Director, Blake Stephens

DEDICATION

To Leo

THE INLET

First Edition

Hank Brooks

CONTENTS

CHAPTER ONE

Whether you are walking down a street, driving down a road, or rowing on some remote secluded mountain lake, you just never know what lies waiting for you; around the corner, around the curve, or on the little inlet you just maneuvered your boat into. The young man, rowing his tiny canoe into the tiny inlet, looked up to see a quaint little cottage in a tree shaded spot on the banks of the lake, and his life was about to change forever.

Andrew Stanley, Esq. was in his fourth year practicing law in his native New York City. He was with the same firm, at the same job, that he had accepted right out of law school, except now he could smell a partnership waiting for him in the not so distant future. He was a very successful attorney, and his life seemed fulfilled, at least on the surface. Andrew had everything except the one thing he longed for the most; someone for him to love and who would most certainly love him back. He was the very definition of a workaholic. He never let up working 24/7. There was no way he would find the love of his life from behind his overburdened desk.

He was recruited on the NYU campus by a young attorney from Miller, Miller and Hengis. Before meeting with their representative, Andrew did some homework. He learned that Miller, Miller and Hengis had been in business a mere ten years, but they were growing exponentially, and were fast evolving from an embryo firm into a promising mid-sized law firm. Anyone joining them at this point in their growth was facing a potentially bright and successful future.

He was interviewed in the conference room of the firm's offices on Madison Avenue. Reggie Kaplan met him in the reception area. Reggie was not much older than Andrew. Indeed, he told Andrew that he had graduated from LIU Law only three years ago. Reggie and Andrew shook hands cordially, and Reggie took Andrew into the conference room.

This was the third, and hopefully last, interview with a law firm that Andrew had endured. When he had walked into the reception area, a warm feeling invaded his body. He felt very much at home. It was as if he was already working here. When the pretty young receptionist smiled at him, he felt as if they were old friends, and when Reggie shook his hand, he felt that he was being welcomed into a warm and loving home, and not so much into a business office.

Even the interview was not quite an interview. The firm had sought him out. They already knew all about his academic achievements, and needed only to learn a little about his personal life.

"My parents are alive and well and live on the upper east side of Manhattan. My dad's a pediatrician. I have one married sister, Sharon. Her husband Thomas is an attorney also, and they live in Oceanside with their two little kids. My brother-in-law practices law on Long Island. He wanted me to join him, but I prefer to stay in The City," Andrew told Reggie.

Then Reggie told Andrew something about the firm. It was founded ten years ago by Frank and Harry Miller, along with Frank's best friend, Brian Hengis. Even though the Miller brothers are one year apart in age, the three founders all graduated from Harvard Law at the same time. They each had enough of a nest egg to be able to afford to start their own firm right after school. They relied on their contacts and on their abilities to achieve success, and apparently they accomplished their goal.

In the ensuing ten years, they all got married and now have children. Andrew already knew how successful the firm was, but Reggie emphasized their phenomenal growth. He encouraged Andrew to ask questions lest he omit something important. As the interview progressed, it became more and more obvious that Andrew would be offered the job and that he would accept.

The interview was about an hour old, when Reggie excused himself. He was only gone a short while, and he returned with a handsome thirty something gentleman. Reggie introduced him to Frank Miller and the two men shook each other's hands with firm grips. Andrew was surprised to see that Frank was not wearing a tie, but he did have on a dress shirt. At the same time, he liked the informality that not wearing a tie hinted at. It gave the impression that the firm was not a stuffy Madison Avenue company. As soon as introductions were made, Reggie shook Andrew's hand, wished him luck, and left the conference room. Frank asked Andrew so few questions that it was obvious that he trusted Reggie's judgment enough to let him make so important a decision on his own.

Of course, Frank was only there to make the offer official and to discuss a starting salary. That was pretty academic, but Andrew's starting date was important to him. There were still six weeks to graduation, and Andrew requested two weeks off after that to study for, and to take, the bar exam.

"Why don't we just say you'll start on July 15th," Frank said.

"Perfect. Thank you so much," Andrew said. With that settled, they chatted cordially for a while, just getting to know each other. Andrew liked Frank. In fact, he liked everybody he had met so far at the firm. Frank took him around to meet his brother, Harry, and the third senior partner, Brian Hengis. He also introduced him to the other associates, the paralegals and the clerical staff. After all the introductions were made, Frank shook Andrew's hand, and he walked Andrew to the elevator.

"I wish you the best of luck, young man," Frank said as the elevator doors opened. "I know you are going to be a real asset to the firm."

As busy as Andrew was during the next two months, whenever he had a few hours to spare, he came to the office without expecting any pay. He helped the other attorneys and the paralegals to do research and he helped them to prepare their briefs. The senior partners were very impressed, and although Andrew did not want, nor did he expect any pay, his first pay check included a bonus of appreciation.

Andrew started on July 15ᵗʰ, and he did not take a vacation or a day off for almost four years. During those years, he had helped the firm grow and he brought in lots of business. Most of the clients he had recruited were gay and owned their own businesses. This did not escape the attention of the senior partners, and they speculated among themselves about Andrew's sexual preference. After all, he was twenty-nine now, and they never knew him to have a serious relationship with a woman. Frank pointed out that they never knew him to have a serious relationship with a man either.

One day Harry Miller knocked on his office door.

"Come in," Andrew said.

"We insist," Harry began without any prelude or small talk, "that you take a couple of weeks off. Look, Andrew, we appreciate you. You have nothing to prove to us. You are an integral part of this firm, but you won't do any of us any good if you continue to work like this without taking some time off. You'll get sick and be useful to nobody."

"But I like to work, and I wouldn't know where to go," Andrew argued.

"I know a quiet lodge in The Catskills," Harry said. "It's about two hours drive from New York and it might as well be at the other end of the earth. It's that isolated. You can refresh yourself and commune with nature all by yourself. That is of course, unless you bring a girlfriend along."

"There's no girlfriend," Andrew answered.

Andrew was liked by everyone in the firm from the senior partners down to the file clerks. He was secure enough in the knowledge of his value to the firm that he had no problem when Harry said to him, "Andrew, I don't mean to pry, and it wouldn't make an iota of difference, but are you gay? Most of your client base seems to be gay."

Without hesitating, Andrew answered, "Yes I am. I suppose I should have said something sooner."

"What for?" Harry asked. "It's not important. I'm not one to put tags and labels on somebody and judge him by those labels. You're a fine man, Andrew, and a damn good lawyer. That's all I care about."

Then he quipped, "Maybe you want to bring a boyfriend on your vacation?"

Without missing a beat, Andrew answered, "No boyfriend either."

"There you go. Now you can see how badly you need this vacation," Harry said.

When Andrew arrived at the lodge that Harry Miller had recommended, it was late May. Most of the lodge bookings would not be there until after Memorial Day, a week away. Andrew was booked for the week before and the week after the holiday. The lodge was practically empty when he checked in. Besides Andrew, there was a honeymoon couple from Buffalo, two spinsters from Syracuse, and one widower from Queens. Andrew learned from the desk clerk that his wife had recently passed away. They had spent two weeks here every summer for as many years as he could remember, and the gentleman did not want to change his plans or cancel the reservation he had made the year before.

The setting of The Waterfall Lodge was magnificent. It sat on the edge of a large crystal clear lake. The lake itself was fed by a magnificent waterfall some one hundred feet wide. The drop to the bottom was approximately fifty feet. Where the rushing waters fell, the lake was deep, turbulent and murky, but where the lake was quiet, it was so clear that you could see a variety of fish. Fishing was allowed to the public only two weeks a year, in the fall, so regretfully, Andrew would not then be allowed to fish.

Andrew was assigned a large corner room with a view of the waterfall. The view delighted him. In spite of the rustic nature of the lodge, the room was very modern. He had a king size bed, which was twice what he had at home, and he looked forward to lounging around in it. Hanging on the wall in front of the bed was a flat screen plasma TV. A DVD player was connected to the TV and sat on the dresser. He also noted that there was internet hookup for his laptop.

What there wasn't a lot of, were things to do. The lodge had a small gym so that Andrew could work out. He could also take long hikes, and if the weather warmed (not likely before Memorial Day) he could swim in the pool. There were also bicycles available should he wish to go biking. The most interesting thing, and new to him, was that he could go rowing. Several rowboats lined the small quay on the lake. Andrew was a city boy. He had never gone rowing, but he vowed to give it a try.

On his first morning at the lodge, immediately after breakfast, he went down to the lake. Each boat had a set of oars inside. Andrew realized that he would have to affix the oars in the oarlocks himself before he could venture out. Before getting into one of the boats, he studied the oarlocks and knew exactly what he had to do. He climbed in gingerly and waited until the boat stopped rocking before he attempted to lock the oars.

When that was accomplished, he put on one of the two life jackets, which he found in the boat. Then he untied the boat and let it drift a little bit before putting the oars in the water. He spent the next fifteen minutes experimenting with the oars until he figured out how to go forward, backwards and how to turn around. When he gained confidence, he ventured out on the lake.

Andrew belonged to a gym and worked out regularly, but he had no idea what a strain he placed on his shoulders and upper body when he was rowing. He suddenly grew very tired and knew he had to rest. He was too far from the lodge to return, but he was close to a shore line. He rowed over to the shore and noted that a slight right turn would put him into a small inlet.

When he turned into the inlet he was pleased to see that there was a small dock where he could moor the boat. He maneuvered the boat to the dock and was able to secure the line. He unlocked the oars and laid them inside the boat. After he removed the life jacket, he climbed out of the boat and onto the dock. Andrew immediately learned the definition of sea legs and land legs. It took him a few unsteady strolls up and down the dock until he got his land legs back.

Once he felt firmly rooted to the ground, he looked around. About a hundred feet from the dock, he saw the little cottage, which he had noticed when he entered the inlet. The back faced the lake, and he could clearly see that there was a road running in front of the cottage, and a late model convertible sat in the driveway. He was afraid that he might be trespassing, so he decided to walk up to the cottage to explain his situation.

He was about halfway from his destination when the back door of the cottage opened and someone came out. Andrew's pulse quickened. The most gorgeous hunk of a man exited the house and started walking toward him. Andrew stopped dead in his tracks. His feet wouldn't move. For just a moment, he was afraid that the man might be angry because he had disturbed his peace. As the man walked toward him, Andrew relaxed. The man was grinning from ear to ear. He was obviously a friendly 'alien' and glad to see another human being. The cottage was so isolated that Andrew almost said, "Take me to your leader." He had to laugh to himself for thinking such a foolish thought.

When the man was about ten feet away, Andrew's jaw dropped open. It was Mike Farrell, his roommate at Syracuse University where he had done his undergraduate work. They had gotten along well enough, but Mike was a jock and Andrew was a bookworm, a nerd, a geek. Mike played for the Syracuse football team, and Andrew was on the debating team. They hadn't had much in common and never really became close friends in the four years they had roomed together.

"My God," Andrew just about screamed. "Mike. Mike Farrell, is that you?"

"Sorry," the man said. "My name is Kyle Farrell. I have a kid brother named Mike. Do you know him?"

"Yes I do," Andrew answered. "Mike was my college roommate. You look enough like him to be his twin."

"Almost," Kyle answered. "I'm only eleven months older than he is." Andrew realized that he and Mike had never been close enough for him to have found out that he had an older brother.

Kyle extended his hand and Andrew shook it. He introduced himself, and suddenly he was filled with emotions, which he thought he had buried years ago.

Andrew was in his room, making up his bed, on his first day at Syracuse University. *When I'm done*, he thought, *I'll organize my closet and my desk and set up my computer. It shouldn't take too long and then I can go explore the campus.* As he was lost in thought and planning his day, his new roommate came in. They introduced themselves and Mike asked Andrew if he would help him unload his car. He was parked illegally in front of the dorm entrance and he wanted to move it as soon as possible.

Andrew didn't answer him and Mike thought that he was kind of rude. Actually, Andrew was in a state of shock. Mike was almost six inches taller than he was and too beautiful for words. He didn't know how he could survive the year without putting a move on this hunk. It turned out that Andrew had to restrain himself for four years.

Andrew came out of his reverie. "Sorry man, sure I'll help."

The two men worked together for the next couple of hours, helping each other out. Once or twice Andrew accidently brushed against Mike in the cramped quarters, and he started to fill out his briefs. When they were done setting up their room, they congratulated each other on how nice it looked, and they went their separate ways. This was to be the pattern for four years. They had nothing in common and neither tried to be more than a considerate roommate.

Although they were both very discreet, it was inevitable that occasionally they saw each other naked. Mike thought nothing of it. He spent half his life in a locker room anyhow, but it was a big deal for Andrew. He had to muster all his strength to remain cool.

Andrew was 5'10" and Mike was 6'4". They were both circumcised. Mike was about 6" flaccid and when Andrew saw his morning woodie the first time, he figured it to be at least 8 and a half inches and very thick. Andrew could only wonder if it got bigger in the heat of sexual passion. Andrew was about 5" flaccid and about 7" hard. He had never been ashamed of his size, but Mike made him feel totally inadequate.

At night he would lie in his bed and imagine what it would be like to have Mike inside of him. He knew he could get all of him up his ass, but he wondered how much of Mike's huge tool he could get down his throat. If Mike was not in the room, Andrew would whack off dreaming that Mike was fucking him. He spilled his seed in a wad of tissues he brought to bed with him. This happened often because Mike usually spent the night with some hot chick. They saw so little of each other, that in four years their conversations were limited to: "How ya doing?" or "Hi there!" Neither knew anything about the other.

Andrew was not exactly celibate either. He knew about a gay bar near the university and was sure his brothers and some sisters hung out there. He declined to go there, preferring to stay in the closet. Instead he went on line and consulted the gay yellow pages. He found a gay bar miles from the campus and one Friday evening he paid it a visit.

He was pleasantly surprised when he went in. There was no loud disco music. Instead, a gentleman, who was at least sixty years old, sat at the piano and played and sang lovely ballads. He particularly favored Cole Porter. There were several stools around the piano bar, and the first time Andrew came to the bar, they were all occupied. In the days to follow, however, he would occupy one seat at the piano bar all night.

The clientele of the bar were generally more mature men. There were a few youngsters like him, but the majority of the patrons ranged in age from about forty and up. Andrew was very mature for his age and intellectually advanced. He had no trouble fitting in. He liked most of the men he met, and was oblivious to the fact that they all lusted after him. On his part, Andrew was falling in love with the piano player.

Sitting at the piano bar every night, he and Tim Jenkins became good friends. Between songs they chatted and learned all about themselves. Tim had been in a relationship for more than twenty five years. His partner died of liver cancer about three years ago. He was very lonely, but wasn't ready for another relationship. "I wouldn't mind a one night stand once in a while," he said to Andrew one evening, with a wink of his eye.

For his part, Andrew admitted that although he had played with a friend in high school, he had never had an adult relationship.

"Don't worry. It'll happen," Tim promised him.

As their friendship grew, they started to have a drink together at the main bar when Tim's gig was over. Andrew savored these moments. For some reason, the two men always had plenty to talk about. They would discuss the latest movies, books they had read and enjoyed, the kind of music they each loved, Tim's late partner, Andrew's aspirations for the future. They were never at a loss for topics of conversation.

One evening as they were chatting away amiably, Tim put his hand on Andrew's knee. It was a spontaneous act. He was hardly aware that he was doing it. Andrew responded by putting his hand on Tim's thigh and then moving it up and down.

Tim grew silent. A tear filled his eye. When Andrew saw the tear, he wiped it away with his finger. "I live walking distance from here," Tim said. "Would you like to come home with me for a cup of coffee? I have some apple pie too."

Andrew nodded. He was more than anxious to go home with Tim and he jumped up from the bar. When he jumped up, Tim did also. He grabbed Andrew's hand and they actually ran to Tim's house.

Tim lived in a private, freestanding house with three bedrooms, a den and a two car garage. He and his late partner had lived there for over twenty years. When they entered the house, Tim closed the door and the two men fell into each other's arms. Their lips parted and they tongued each other sensually.

"This can't be happening," Tim whispered.

"Ah but it is," Andrew assured him. Tim grabbed Andrew's hand again and led him to the bedroom. They undressed quickly, allowing their clothes to drop to the floor. Andrew could not believe how nice a body Tim had. Except that his ass sagged ever so slightly, the rest of him could have been the body of a much younger man. Tim caught Andrew giving his ass the once over. "After all," he said, "I am sixty-two."

Forty-three years separated the two men who were about to make love. "What does it matter?" Andrew said. "You look great to me."

"I must warn you," Tim said. "I'll get hard, but not quite hard enough to fuck. But if you would fuck me, I'd die a happy man." He said that so seriously that Andrew was surprised when Tim started to laugh. He also took a good look at Tim's cock. Tim was erect, but Andrew could see that it was a soft erection. He could care less. Tim was about the same size he was, and he couldn't wait to get that luscious cock inside his mouth. Tim was not very hairy, but a light gray fur covered the middle of his chest and fused into his pubic hair. Andrew thought that was very sexy. Excess hair did not turn him on.

Tim being the older of the two assumed it was his responsibility to get the ball rolling. He asked Andrew to lie on his back and he lowered himself on to the younger man. They were both erect and he made sure that their cock's ground together as he began to kiss the nubile young man. After a while, his lips wandered down to Andrew's right ear. He darted in and out of the ear and swabbed all around it. Andrew was already close to shooting his load. Somehow, Tim sensed that Andrew's relief was near and he stopped playing with his ear.

His tongue found Andrew's tits and he sucked on both of them alternately. Andrew squealed in delight, and was glad that he had chosen an older man with lots of experience for his first real gay sexual encounter.

He became aware that Tim was now sucking on his innie. He sucked as if he had a straw in his mouth, and was trying to convert the innie into an outie. By now Andrew's squealing was growing louder. He was anticipating Tim reaching his cock at last, but he was in for a temporary disappointment. When Tim was finished playing with Andrew's belly button, he rolled him over.

Andrew could feel Tim's feathery fingers kneading up and down his back and finally engulfing his ass cheeks. Tim squeezed the cheeks and then started to spread them. In a short while, Andrew could feel Tim's tongue running up and down his crack and for a moment he thought that Tim had entered his ass hole, but he wasn't sure. Then there it was again. Tim was indeed sucking his asshole and occasionally entering it with his tongue.

Then a new sensation caressed Andrew's body. Tim had inserted a greasy finger into Andrew's hole. When had he lubed it? Andrew was not aware of when, nor did he care. Tim had found Andrew's prostate and was massaging it gently. When Andrew's balls began to constrict, Tom stopped everything he was doing. He went to a dresser drawer and pulled out a condom. He rolled Andrew over, pulled the condom down on his cock, and then lubricated it. He got into bed and lay flat on his back.

"Fuck me, please," he begged.

Instinctively Andrew got up and stood between Tim's legs. He raised Tim's legs and started to enter him.

"Yes, yes," Tim moaned. "Slowly, just like that. "It's been so long. This feels so good." Tim was crying and tears ran down his cheeks. Andrew was too young to control his orgasm and he came way too soon. His cock had been teasing Tim's prostate and Tim was close to cumming also, but no cigars yet. Andrew's fading cock slipped out of Tim's ass. He pulled off the condom and threw it in the toilet.

He got back in bed and lay side by side next to Tim. He reached over and began to fondle Tim's tool. As soon as he was able to breathe again, he went down on Tim and started sucking him slowly and with great passion. It had been a long time for Tim too, and he came way too fast also. Andrew swallowed most of Tim's cum and then kissed him and they shared what was left.

Tim and Andrew became weekend sex warriors until toward the end of Andrew's junior year. During those years, it was easy to resist the alluring Mike Farrell. He just projected that he would be with Tim soon enough. One night Andrew went home with Tim after his gig. For the first time since they began to have sex together, Tim did not undress quickly or head to the bedroom. He made them coffee instead and sat at the kitchen table with Andrew. He took Andrew's hands in his and said very sadly.

"Andrew, my love, we have to end this. I've met a man who is my age and a widower like me. We really hit it off and we both want to end our loneliness. He's moving in with me very soon. I truly love you. You saved my life, but we both know that you'll be leaving soon and that forty three years is way too much difference. You need a younger man."

"Can we make love one more time?" Andrew pleaded.

"It will be harder to part."

"I don't care."

When Andrew stopped seeing Tim, the sexual tension in his dorm room increased more than it ever had. It took all of his strength and will power to keep from attacking Mike. He would dream of going down on Mike while Mike was sleeping, or crawling into bed with him and masturbating him. Somehow, he managed never to do any of those things, and to graduate without once touching Mike.

CHAPTER TWO

"A penny for your thoughts," Kyle offered. "You seem to be a million miles away."

"Sorry," Andrew said trying to recover himself. "It's just that you look so much like Mike, I got transported back to good old Syracuse University."

"I went to Buffalo myself," Kyle said.

So that's why we never met, Andrew mused.

"Are you staying at The Waterfall Lodge?" Kyle asked.

"Uh huh," Andrew nodded.

"Don't tell me. You rowed out too far and your arms gave out. It happens all the time. You're welcome to come inside. I'll make some coffee until you feel ready to go again."

"I'd like that," Andrew said.

The cottage consisted of a kitchen, a bathroom, a bedroom, and a living room. There was a small TV in the living room and a combination DVD and CD player were attached to it. All in all, it seemed like a cozy get away place.

Almost as if he could read Andrew's inquisitive mind, Kyle said, "I teach English and American Lit at SUNY Albany. A couple of years ago I bought this place for a song. It's close enough to Albany that I can escape here most weekends, and when school is out, I can spend as much time as I want to here. The spring semester ended last Friday, and voila, here I am."

"I'm a lawyer and I work pretty much seven days a week," Andrew lamented. "This is my first time off in four years, and it was bosses' orders."

"Doesn't sound like you have much of a social life," Kyle commented.

Andrew was rather insulted by that remark. He didn't feel that one's social life should be judged by how much one works.

"None at all, thank you very much. Somehow, I don't think you should be critical, Kyle. If you spend all your free time here, when do you have time for a social life?" Andrew could not wait to hear Kyle's answer to his question.

Almost as if he was back in the dorm room with Mike, Andrew's cock began to stiffen. Kyle was even more attractive than Mike was. Andrew reasoned that he found him more attractive because he was not a kid anymore, like Mike had been back then. He was a mature professor of literature.

"I just haven't found anyone I want to socialize with. If I ever do, it will have to be someone who'll want to share this haven with me. Can you imagine two people enjoying romantic evenings here?" Kyle asked.

He meant the question to be rhetorical, but Andrew answered, "I sure can, Kyle." He was glad he was seated because his cock grew a little bit bigger. He thought back to what Tim had told him. *Don't worry. It'll happen.* But every time he felt a longing for someone, that someone turned out to be straight. Well, he knew that he couldn't spend too much more time alone here with Kyle or he would tip his hand, and probably get beaten to a pulp.

He stood to leave. "Thanks for the coffee," he said. "I'd better get going."

"Please don't go," Kyle said. "It's not that I get lonely, but you are the first person I have ever wanted to share this place with. Spend the day and have dinner with me. I've got plenty of food. I have a rack on my car. We can load the boat on it and I can take you back after dinner.

Andrew's hormones were working overtime and he was getting harder. He had to sit down again. Kyle must have noticed. "I'd like to stay, really I would, but they would miss me at the lodge and maybe send out a search party. I never gave them my cell phone number."

"There you go," Kyle said and his face actually registered relief. "You can call them, and tell them you'll be back late. At the same time you can give them your cell phone number." As much as Andrew believed that the better part of valor was a hasty retreat, he could not resist the urgent way that Kyle asked him to stay.

"You win," he said. He whipped out his cell phone, but there were no bars in this remote spot.

"I guess I'll have to go after all," he said.

"You aren't getting out of it that easily," Kyle said. "I have a land phone."

Part of Andrew said, "Shit," and the other part said, "Thank you God."

Kyle pointed to the phone. In order to use it, Andrew would have to stand and walk over to it. He suspected that Kyle had already noticed that he was hard. If he stood now, his hardness would be confirmed. No matter what awful things he tried to think about, his erection would not subside. Instantly, he made a decision. He would stand up and expose the obvious. If it offended Kyle, he could still leave. If Kyle did not react, he would just have to wait and see what would happen. After all, so far Kyle was more anxious for him to stay than he was.

He stood up and turned toward the phone. His erection was ripping at his jeans and obvious to even the most casual observer. What happened next had previously happened only in his fantasies.

Kyle gave out a low whistle. "Nice," he murmured. "I'd appreciate it if you made that call quickly. Maybe you should say that you'll be back tomorrow morning."

The two men smiled at each other and Andrew made the call. He gave Kyle's number to the lodge. When he hung up the phone, he looked at Kyle's smiling face. "What now?" he asked.

"Right now," Kyle answered, I'd like to rip your clothes off and fuck your brains out. But honestly, Andy (nobody ever called Andrew, Andy, and if they did he corrected them, but coming from Kyle it sounded just right) I don't want this to be a one night stand. Could we just sit and talk for a while and get to know each other?"

Andrew remembered the number of weeks that he and Tim had talked and talked before Tim ventured to put his hand on Andrew's knee. "You bet," he said. "It's a great idea."

Kyle took Andrew's hand and led him to the sofa in the living room. They removed their sneakers, and Kyle sat Andrew down facing away from him, so that in the end Andrew's back was leaning against Kyle's chest. Kyle put his arms around Andrew and drew him close, but he never let his arms wander further down than Andrew's chest.

"Did you and my brother ever make it together?" Kyle wanted to know.

"Surely you jest, big guy," Andrew laughed. "I spent four years trying not to touch him. It was desperately hard work. And here I sit now, with his clone, and we are holding each other. If this doesn't prove that dreams can come true, I don't know what does."

"When did you first know that you were gay?" Kyle asked.

"Shit. In middle school, I think. I came out to a friend's uncle at the same time my friend did. In high school I used to whack off with that friend. I loved it, but we never touched each other, and after a while we just stopped doing it. I never had sex with a guy until college. I finally came out to my folks before I left for college. My father is a doctor." Andrew started to laugh.

"Why are you laughing?" Kyle asked.

"You know what he said to me? He said, 'That's cool, son. As long as your sister makes me a grandfather, I don't care.' It was one week after my sister's wedding."

"Tell me about your college days and your first experience?"

Andrew told him all about Tim. "There's a lot to be said for an older man," Andrew added. "He had the experience to know just how to make a guy happy. I learned a lot from him."

"Glad to hear that," Kyle said with a leer. "And you have been celibate since?"

Andrew nodded. "Uh huh," he said. "I have had occasional one night stands, but it's been a while now."

"Unbelievable," Kyle mumbled.

"How about you?" Andrew asked "I want to know everything."

Kyle's family lived in Rochester, NY. His father owned a drug store. He was forced to close the store a few years ago because he could not compete with the big chain stores springing up all around him. He now worked for one of those chains, and made a better salary than when he was a sole proprietor. Kyle's mother taught at the local elementary school. The worst experience of his young life was when his mother was his teacher. The other kids razzed him unmercifully. "Teacher's pet," they constantly yelled at him in the school yard.

He, and his only brother, Mike, were inseparable. Kyle was a year ahead of Mike in school. He once contemplated flunking on purpose so that they could be in the same grade. In the end, he thought better of it. He was a better student than Mike and he didn't want his teachers comparing them academically. They were both jocks, and although Kyle was great at sports, Mike was the real talent.

The two boys shared a room, and as often as they had seen each other naked, the teen age male hormones have a way of changing everything. One night, when Kyle was fifteen, he came home late. He entered their room as silently as possible. As usual, Mike was sleeping naked. He was on his back and he had an erection that was immense. Kyle had never realized how well-endowed his brother was. The strangest feeling came over him. He wanted to bend down, take Mike in his mouth and suck the juices out of him. He got so scared he ran to the bathroom and took a cold shower.

Kyle had heard of homosexuality, but it was an abstract concept to him. He didn't know any homos or queers or whatever they were called, and besides he was told that homos go to hell when they die. He successfully wiped any thoughts that he might be gay, right out of his head. He was even able to ogle his brother and remain flaccid merely by picturing the fires of hell. In spite of that strong resolve, he rarely dated girls. He did get a date for his senior prom, and he fucked her that very night because it was expected. It was his first time. It was a nice experience but that was the moment he allowed himself to admit that he would rather fuck a guy. His date fondled him and he managed to get semi erect, but in order for him to get an erection sufficient for fucking, he began to fantasize that he was being fondled by his football coach. He had long dreamed of being fucked by Mr. Saunders in the locker room, in front of the whole football team. That got him so turned on; his date labeled him a tiger.

Once he arrived at The University of Buffalo, some of his constraints vanished. In Buffalo, he heard about a gay bar called *University Heights*. It was right outside the campus, so he wouldn't even have to go downtown for action. By this time his yearnings were becoming unbearable obsessions. He wanted to have male sex so badly he made a pact with himself that he would pay for it if necessary.

Kyle did not realize how handsome he was. The first time he entered the bar, he was beset with guys who wanted him badly. That very first night he went home with a senior who lived off campus, and who could 'entertain' guests freely. The senior was experienced and quite adept in the art of male love. He made Kyle's first experience a real whopper. After that first time, Kyle only went to the bar when he could no longer control his urges, which was pretty often. He scored every time.

One Saturday morning, Kyle headed for the showers. His roommate was close behind him. They showered in silence and returned to their room wrapped only in a towel. When they entered the room, Kyle's roommate, Bob, closed and locked the door. Then he ripped the towel off of Kyle. Kyle was shocked to say the least.

"Have you got something you'd like to confess to me?" Bob asked. Kyle heard warning bells clanging throughout his body.

"What do you mean?" he asked. He got his naked self into Bob's face in a subconscious effort to use his bulky frame to scare the shit out of Bob.

"Relax, Kyle," Bob said, and he grabbed Kyle around the neck and started to kiss him.

Kyle was too shocked to do anything but allow it to happen. Soon nature worked its wiles and Kyle was kissing back.

"I saw you last night at *University Heights*," Bob said. "I made sure you didn't see me. When I saw you leave with that hot dude, I got really jealous. Imagine that? I got jealous. Please make love to me. I am so hot for you that I leave this room every day with a raging case of blue balls. It's your duty to cure your roommate."

Kyle looked at his roommate and smiled tenderly at him. After that, they made love as often as possible until they graduated. Bob especially loved anal sex and to get fucked. Kyle was eager to oblige. But every so often he insisted that Bob fuck him. It was only fair. Neither of them gave up going to *University Heights*, and usually went home with a different partner. Occasionally they took someone back to their dorm room and enjoyed a threesome.

After graduation, Kyle went to Columbia University in New York to earn a master's degree and then a doctorate in English and American Literature. Bob went to UCLA to earn a law degree. They wrote for a while but eventually lost touch. As sexually active as Kyle had been as an undergraduate, he became very much a loner at Columbia and rarely had sex. Instead, he immersed himself in his studies and his doctoral thesis.

After getting his PhD, Kyle began to teach at SUNY Albany. As much as he hungered after some of his male students, and many came on to him, he knew better than to sleep with any of them. The main reason that he bought the cottage was to get away from them and to minimize temptation. Like Andrew, he was getting very little nookie and he was one hot dude.

When he laid eyes on Andrew, his heart began to race and when he found out that Andrew had been Mike's roommate in college, he could hardly contain himself. Mike had told him that he was almost certain that his roommate was gay, but he was too shy to ask. Mike thought that Andrew and Kyle would like each other.

"So," Kyle said, "now you know all about me, and we're both up to date."

"What's Mike doing?" Andrew asked.

"Wow, you really are a workaholic if you don't know that Mike plays football for The New York Jets. He's married and has two kids, a boy and a girl. I spoil them silly, and I'm their favorite uncle. They have another uncle on their mother's side."

"Does Mike know you're gay?"

"Oh sure. The fucker once told me that he purposely used to get hard in our bedroom to tease me. We love each other, Andy. Nothing can change that. When we were in college, do you know what he once said to me? He said that he suspected that his roommate was gay and he would love to get us together. He thought we would make a great pair. It never happened because he wasn't sure about you and he would never ask."

"Do you think we have talked enough, and gotten to know enough about each other?" Andrew asked.

To answer the question, Kyle's arms went slowly down Andrew's body until his hand wrapped around Andrew's package. Andrew sighed deeply and turned around to face Kyle. Their lips met and they started out with light kisses, but as their yearning grew, their kisses became more passionate.

Kyle stood up and grabbed Andrew's hand, pulling him off the sofa. Their lips met again and their tongues began to caress. All the while they were kissing; Kyle was leading Andrew into the bedroom. When they got there they began to unbutton each other's flannel shirts with fumbling hands. They took off their shirts and let them drop to the floor. Andrew's hands found one of Kyle's nipples and he began to pinch it. A moan of pleasure escaped from Kyle's throat. Then Andrew pinched the other nipple.

While he was playing with Kyle's tits, Kyle was unbuckling Andrew's belt. Andrew stopped playing with Kyle's hairless chest and began to unbuckle his belt also. They let their jeans drop to the floor, and they stepped out of them. All they each had on now were jockey shorts and crew socks. The bulges in their shorts gave promise of two well-endowed young men.

Suddenly Kyle dropped to his knees. He grabbed the elastic waist band of Andrew's briefs with his teeth, and slowly maneuvered the shorts down and onto Andrew's thighs. He was rewarded with a hard seven inch cock flapping about his face. He started to lick up and down the luscious cock. Kyle pulled the shorts the rest of the way down and Andrew stepped out of them. Kyle rose and removed his briefs and his socks. Andrew removed his socks and examined Kyle. His cock was just as big and fat as Mike's and Andrew almost fainted in anticipation.

They got into bed and lay facing each other. Their arms entwined their torsos, and their cocks ground together. They kissed and rubbed their cocks together. "I'm in paradise," Andrew whispered in Kyle's ear.

"What's beyond paradise?" Kyle asked. "That's where I intend to send you." He rolled over and was lying on top of Andrew. He was kissing so passionately that Andrew could hardly bear it. Kyle was 6'4" tall and weighed 220 pounds. Andrew was 5'10" tall and weighed 165 pounds. Kyle should have been crushing Andrew's bones, but miraculously Andrew did not find Kyle heavy at all.

"Suck me and then fuck me," Andrew pleaded.

Kyle answered by asking a question. "Will you do the same to me? My college roommate wanted me to fuck him all the time, and I had to beg him to reciprocate."

"Don't be a jerk," Andrew answered. "I'll do anything you want me to. All my fantasies are coming true."

With that promise having been made, Kyle began to slither down Andrew's body. Andrew was as hairless as Kyle except that he had a good amount of hair around his nipples. On the way down, he kept kissing Andrew's body, but he went straight for Andrew's cock. He was too hungry to waste time. He reckoned that in the future he could linger longer on other parts of Andrew's body. He was certain that there would be a future. In one gulp he enveloped Andrew's cock. His tongue began to run up and down the underside of Andrew's tool. At the same time, one of Kyle's hands was nipping Andrew's nipples alternately, while his other hand played with Andrew's balls fondling them like a feather duster.

"I'm cumming," Andrew suddenly yelled. "Please don't stop. We'll fuck later."

Later!!!! Kyle exulted at the word, and he sucked harder. He could feel Andrew's cum rising through his cock and finally it reached its destination. Kyle lost count of the number of spurts that descended down his throat. He just kept swallowing and swallowing as tears flowed out of his eyes. He held Andrew in his mouth until the precious cock grew limp. Only then did he surrender his prize.

They lay side by side for a while, squeezing their hands. Finally, Kyle said. "Please don't be frightened and please don't run away. I have something to tell you. Andy, beloved Andy, I fell in love with you the moment I saw you. I was exultant when I found out you were Mike's roommate because he told me that he suspected you were gay." Kyle giggled. "My straight brother has pretty decent gaydar don't you think? Are you OK with what I just said to you?"

Andrew answered by saying, "You can fuck me now big guy, but be gentle. That's a pretty hefty rod to take, you know."

Kyle opened the top drawer of his night table. "I use this when I whack off," he said, removing a jar of Vaseline. Andrew was on his back so Kyle placed a pillow under his buttocks and began lubing Andrew's ass. As he did so, he reamed it a little to stretch it.

"I have no rubbers," Kyle apologized. "But I swear I have been with very few guys since my undergraduate days, and I always used protection."

"Same here," Andrew swore. "I guess that makes it OK to go bareback, and we'll both enjoy it more."

Kyle greased up his throbbing, monstrous cock and placed it at Andrew's opening. Andrew raised his legs and Kyle began to enter slowly. He was doing well for a little bit until he reached Andrew's sphincter. At that point Andrew jumped and Kyle stopped.

"Don't stop," Andrew begged. "Drive it in all the way, then don't move. Like removing a band aid, it's best to give one strong yank."

"Are you sure?"

"Yes, please just do it. Andrew put a fist in his mouth, and Kyle battered in. When he was all the way in, he stayed perfectly still. Andrew bit his fist so hard, he drew a little blood. The pain was excruciating, but he bore it because he wanted this so badly. With his mammoth cock firmly implanted, Kyle leaned over Andrew and began to kiss him and pinch his tits. Andrew's pain seemed to lessen, slowly at first and then more rapidly. After a while there was no pain at all. Andrew had a warm sensation of having his whole body filled with Kyle's love.

"It's OK to begin stroking now, but start slowly," he informed Kyle. Kyle did just that but little by little he pumped harder as he felt his moment in paradise building. Andrew began to yell, "Harder, love, harder." Kyle obliged Andrew's wishes as he achieved orgasm. Kyle could not remember such an orgasm ever before. It seemed to be forming in his toes and expanding throughout his entire body as he pumped stream after stream into Andrew's ass. Finally, he collapsed in a heap onto his lover's body. He remained that way until his cock went limp. For most men, that would be the point where a limp dick would fall out of a lover's ass, but not so for Kyle. He was so big that limp as it was, his cock remained inside of Andrew. For his part, Andrew was loathe to release it. For the first time in months, Andrew thought of Tim, and promised himself to call Tim and tell him about Kyle. He knew how pleased Tim would be.

At long last, Kyle pulled out, rolled over and lay side by side with Andrew. He reached over and engulfed Andrew's flaccid package with his massive hand. Andrew began to get an erection again, and Kyle continued to fondle him. Andrew rolled over on his side, so Kyle did the same. Their lips met and finally Andrew said, "I love you too." He then fell asleep in Kyle's arms. Kyle kissed Andrew's forehead and he fell asleep also.

When Andrew awoke he instinctively reached over to Kyle, but he was alone in bed. He looked around. The sun was very low in the sky. The evening of his first day in paradise was about to begin. He called out to Kyle but there was no answer. The cottage was totally isolated from most of the world, so he had no trouble getting out of bed naked.

Kyle was nowhere to be seen. Andrew had not previously noticed a sliding glass door at the rear of the living room. He looked out, and there was Kyle barbequing some steaks on the back porch. He was fully dressed, and was even wearing a sweater. Andrew put his hand on the glass door. It was ice cold. It must have gotten really cold out there, so Andrew went back to the bedroom and got dressed. He looked in the closet and saw a windbreaker hanging there. He put it on and it was several sizes too big, but he rolled up the sleeves and ventured out on the porch.

"Pretty cold for late May," he said to Kyle as he planted a kiss on his cheek. Kyle smiled, turned to Andrew, and gave him a proper kiss on the lips, with a little tongue thrown in for good measure.

"Take over the barbeque, will you please?" Kyle asked. I want to open some canned vegetables and I have some bread in the freezer. The steaks should be just about ready by the time I have the table set and everything ready for our first festive meal together."

Together, Andrew thought. *What a beautiful word.*

"How do you like your steak done?" Andrew asked before Kyle could get away.

"Medium."

"Me too," Andrew said.

Andrew tended the steaks, and when they seemed just right, he started into the cottage to get a platter, but Kyle walked out with a platter in hand. Andrew placed the steaks on the platter and followed Kyle back into the kitchen. The table was set for two. The veggies were in a bowl with a serving spoon. The bread was in a bread basket and butter was on the table. What Andrew did not expect to see were the two glasses of red wine and two candles burning seductively on the table.

"You have a truly romantic soul," Andrew said, praising Kyle.

"Let's make it really romantic," Kyle said, and he quickly shed all his clothes except his underwear. Andrew did not waste a second following suit.

They sat down at the table and Kyle raised his wine glass. Andrew did the same. "To us," Kyle said. "May this be the first day of the happiest years of our lives. Happy, because we'll be together."

There, Andrew exulted. *He said it again—together.*

Before either of them could take a sip of the wine, two men burst in on them with guns aimed directly at their faces.

CHAPTER THREE

Joey and Carl Barkin were identical twin brothers. They lived on the lower east side of Manhattan. Their father deserted them when they were not quite two years old, forcing their mother to sell herself on the streets to make ends meet. She had no other skills. Usually she brought her johns home and told the boys not to disturb her as she took her trade into her bedroom. The boys were instructed to stay in their room and not to come out until she called them. Of course they peeked through the keyhole often enough, and by the age of five they knew how a penis and vagina were meant to be used, i.e., for profit.

Mary Barkin was not a bad sort. She had no other choice but to do what she did. She neither drank nor used drugs, and even if she wanted to smoke, she could not afford the price of cigarettes. She provided her boys with food, clothing, shelter and nothing else. By the time they were fifteen, they were running drugs for a dealer and making more money in a week than their mother had made in the past year. Using their new found wealth, they convinced their mother to stop hooking. And just in time. She was beginning to lose her youth and her good looks, and tricks were getting harder and harder to come by. She was only capable of attracting drunkards and drug addicts who were high on cocaine, crack or heroin. Once she stopped soliciting, the boys sent her to a trade school, and she learned secretarial skills. She actually got a job as a secretary for a stock broker. Little by little she regained some of her good looks as she paid more and more attention to her grooming. The stock broker even took her out to dinner when they worked late, but he never made a move on her.

The boys were truly street wise. They knew that they should never take drugs themselves or they would start a sharp descent into a deep abyss aimed straight to hell. The dealer tried hard enough to get them hooked, but to no avail.

They delivered steadily for the dealer until they were nineteen, and then they got entrapped by a narco cop. Mary got them out on bail, but eventually they were each sentenced to 5 to 7 years for possession. They never revealed the source of their stash, thereby earning major brownie points with the dealer and his boss. At the prison, the guard who processed them was smitten by their youthful and innocent good looks. He allowed the brothers to share a cell, figuring that they could look after each other. He had no doubt they would be claimed and raped immediately by the older, tougher inmates, but as a pair, he hoped that they had a fighting chance. What he didn't know was that the dealer's boss had begun to feel very fatherly toward the twins over the years they had worked for him. He sent out word to the prison information network that the boys were out of bounds, and anyone who touched them would be "touched" by him. Nobody ever tried to abuse them, even if the boys would have encouraged it.

They had been sent to prison at the height of their sexual urges. On the streets, they fucked plenty of women. Their good looks served them well. Most of the women wanted both of them together. After all, it was exciting for them to do twins. It was going to be tough for them to get by in prison doing without the women they had been fucking regularly.

During their first night in prison, they lay on separate cots. At some point Joey could hear Carl sobbing. It was obvious that Carl was trying to stifle his cries. Joey got out of bed and lay down with Carl on the tiny cot. They could only manage to share the cot by nesting together like spoons. Carl could feel Joey's cock pressing against his ass and he pushed tighter against his brother. Somehow, it gave him comfort.

After another day or two, they agreed to whack off to relieve the tension. They lay on their separate cots and accomplished the deed.

Neither could tell you how it started, but along the way, they started to talk dirty to each other as they brought themselves to a pleasurable conclusion.

"My cock is so beautiful," Carl intoned. "You would love it if you sucked it.

Joey would then answer. "My asshole is so inviting. You would love it if you fucked it."

They would keep going like that until they came, each inviting the other to invade the other's body. Finally one night Joey said, "I am so hot and horny, bro. Let me jerk you off tonight."

"Great Carl answered. We'll do each other." They didn't expect to enjoy doing each other as much as they did, but after the first time it was the usual way for them to get themselves off.

Now they weren't dummies. They knew what the dominant men in this prison did to their bitches. In every case, the bitch resisted it at first, but in the end they couldn't wait to give their daddy pleasure, because the pleasure was also theirs. Often at night they could hear the bitches giving head and the moans of pure pleasure came from both parties. Nobody spoke of it, but sometimes the daddies fell in love with their bitches and reversed roles. Of course, they weren't stupid enough to get caught doing that and so it remained just a rumor.

One evening, the twins were sitting on Carl's cot comforting each other. Carl was just about to cum and Joey stopped stroking. "Why'd ya stop?" Carl asked, very perturbed.

"We have a long way to go in this dump," Joey explained. "I love you more than myself and I want you to be happy so I want to try something. I don't say I'll like it, and it might be a one-time shot, but here goes." He leaned over and took Carl's dick into his mouth. He wasn't quite sure how to properly suck a cock, but he avoided letting his teeth touch his brother, and he started sucking like he used to suck a lollipop when he was a kid.

Carl was not prepared for the warm, moist feeling he was receiving from his brother. "Oh my God," he moaned. "Oh my God. This is better than a whack job. Better by a country mile." Joey stopped for a moment and said, "I have to admit it, Bro, you taste real good." Then he went down on Carl again. Carl could not contain himself and he came too fast to warn Joey, who got a mouthful of cum. Carl was shocked. He expected Joey to spit it out, but he was swallowing all of it.

"It tasted pretty good, a little sweet, a little salty," Joey announced. "I really liked it. It made me feel very connected to you and I always want us to be that way."

"Then let me connect to you also," Carl whispered and he went down on Joey. When Joey came, barely able to stifle his screams, Carl swallowed all his cum just as his brother had done. That night as they shared one cot, they did something that they had never done before. When Joey said goodnight, he kissed Carl on the lips. Carl kissed back, but with a slightly open mouth. Before they knew it, their kisses became passionate. Their tongues were exploring deep into the other's mouths, and their manhood was at full attention once again. As they kissed and fondled each other, they both came again in each other's palms.

Carl said, "Joey, that was better than with any of the chicks I ever made it with. I love you." He snuggled up to his brother and fell asleep.

Every day in the prison they heard daddies telling whoever would listen about the joys of fucking their bitches in the ass. The shocking part was how often the bitches described how good their daddies made them feel when they were getting fucked. It was just a matter of time before the twins decided to have a go at it.

Joey called his mother and said that kitchen duty had left his hands rough and chapped. He asked her to bring a jar of Vaseline on her next visit. Mary was happy to oblige. The twins could not wait for lights out the evening of her visit. As soon as they were able, they flipped a coin. Carl won and elected to fuck his brother first and then Joey could fuck him. They spent a lot of time lubricating Joey's ass and Carl's cock. Still at the moment of truth, Joey said it hurt too much and made Carl stop trying.

"I've heard the bitches say that it always hurts at first, but it's worth the effort. Once you get used to it, it feels great. Please let's try again," Carl said. "I've got an idea. This time sit on me and lower yourself on my cock, instead of me trying to force my way in."

"OK," Joey said and he squatted over Carl. Carl guided his cock until it was exactly under Joey's opening and told Joey to start sitting a little at a time. I guess this position suited them because Carl entered Joey almost effortlessly. When Joey could not lower himself anymore, he just sat still, not knowing what to do. Carl began to push up into his brother. Joey picked up the rhythm and began to push down when Carl pushed up. They didn't know anything about the prostate, but Joey was getting a full massage. They were both shocked when they came simultaneously. Joey was reluctant to disengage from his brother, but Mother Nature helped him along.

"Jeezus Carl," he said. "It's getting better and better. He kissed his brother and said, "Let's reverse it tomorrow night. I'm too bushed tonight." They fell asleep.

They were released for good behavior after four years, and they were assigned the same parole officer. Mary said that she would pick them up and take them to buy some new clothes before heading home. They were pretty surprised when Mary arrived in a brand new Lexus being driven by a rather nice looking gentleman. The twins knew immediately that this was no pimp. Mary introduced the boys to John DeRosa, her boss. Then she announced that she and John had gotten married just the week before and John said that the boys could stay with them until they got on their feet.

The twins were genuinely happy for their mother, and grateful to their stepfather for his generous offer to two strangers. Unfortunately, things did not go as well as they would have liked. It is difficult enough for ex-cons to find employment, but these two had not even graduated high school and had no skills. After trying to find work for several months, they were definitely outliving their welcome. John did not have to say anything to them. They realized themselves that it was time to leave their mother to her happy new life.

They rented a room in their old neighborhood and sought out their former dealer. They learned that he was out of business so they decided to go right to the big boss, Sam Gardini, and ask him for their old jobs back. He was really happy to have them back. He had protected them in prison without their knowledge, and he still felt very fatherly towards them. During their probation period, he gave them only the simplest and safest jobs, but once the parole officer was out of the picture, the jobs got tougher, but now Sam was paying them a lot more money for their efforts.

He trusted them as he would have trusted his own sons. One day he called them into his office. "Here are the keys to a rented Cadillac that you'll find on the street outside. It's leased to a phony person using a forged driver's license," he said. "There's almost a million dollars in heroin in the trunk." He handed Joey a piece of paper. "These are the directions to an abandoned lot in Englewood, NJ. When you get there, Vinny Montana will be waiting. I don't know how many goons, he'll have with him, but don't worry. He wouldn't dare mess with me. You give him the stash, and he'll hand over a briefcase with money. Just peek in and make sure it's real money. Don't waste time counting. If he short changes me, he's dead. He'll want to test the stash. When he's finished wasting his time and yours, get out of there quick and come straight home."

The twins nodded and ran to the Cadillac. They secured their hidden pistols to their belts, *just in case*. They also made sure that they both had their switch blades in their pockets. Even though they didn't anticipate trouble, it didn't hurt to be prepared. On the way to New Jersey, Joey said, "We could live like kings forever with a million bucks."

"Don't even think about it," Carl said. We wouldn't live long enough to spend it."

"He has to catch us first. With the money, we could buy a ratty old used car, and dump the Cadillac. Buffalo is the second largest city in New York State. We could get lost there. We could even get lost in Syracuse or Rochester or even Albany. We could rent a place under phony names, and since we don't have to work, he would never find us."

"I don't know about that," Carl sounded leery. "He has contacts everywhere."

"If we don't let anyone see us together, we could even pass as one person. One of us can rent an apartment as a single individual while the other lies low. They would be looking for twins and they wouldn't get a lead anywhere on a single guy living alone. We could make it work. Are you with me?"

"I'm scared, Joe," Carl whined, "but I'll do it if that's what you want."

Joe embraced Carl and kissed him on the lips Then he headed the car towards The George Washington Bridge and New Jersey.

The exchange was made effortlessly and the twins were on their way out of the abandoned lot rather quickly. They drove into Englewood and cruised around until they spotted a used car dealer. They left the rental car a couple of blocks from the dealership. The salesman was shocked at how quickly the sale was made, and even more shocked when the buyers said that they would pay cash for a two year old Plymouth. While he was preparing the paper work, Joey went into the washroom and withdrew the required amount of cash from the briefcase. It hardly made a dent. They were out of there in less than two hours and headed to the Palisades Parkway.

At the end of the Parkway, they veered off onto the old Route 9 and headed upstate. They decided not to use the New York State Thruway, but to stick to back roads. They were only about an hour from Kyle's cottage when they began to crow. They were feeling pretty cocky, and began singing and feeling each other's packages. The little fucks had no idea that Sam Gardini already had the make, model, color, year and license plate number of the car that they were driving in.

When Carl and Joey didn't return on time, Sam sent some of his men to Englewood. They quickly found the rental car just a short distance from the used car dealer. On a hunch they found the dealership. A few measly dollars was all the incentive the dealer needed to give Sam's men the information they wanted. Within minutes, the word went out to Sam's extensive network throughout the states of New York and New Jersey. A watch was established at all small and major roads leading into all the main cities. Even the cops on Sam's payroll were on the alert.

Joey and Carl were navigating the most deserted back road they could find. It was beginning to get dark and they were hungry, but they didn't want to stay in a hotel and they didn't come across any restaurants on this rural road.

"Look," Joey said, "Up ahead. I see lights. It looks like a little cabin. Maybe we can confiscate a little food."

They cut their headlights and drove up to the cabin. They crept up to the cabin, and Joey stood guard while Carl peeked in through the window. He started to giggle.

"What do you see?" Joey asked.

"Two fags in their underwear having dinner. This is going to be so easy."

They drew their guns and burst into the cottage. The door wasn't even locked. It was all so sudden that Kyle and Andrew weren't even sure what was happening for a few seconds. Kyle knew that he could easily overpower both of them, but a gun pointing in his face demanded more patience.

"Stand up," Joey commanded. "Keep your gun on them," he said to Carl. He began to ransack the cabin. He was going through the pantry when Carl heard him cry out exultantly, "Perfect!"

Joey had found Kyle's tackle box and it contained plenty of fishing reel wire. He removed it and commanded Kyle and Andrew to turn around. First he tied their hands behind their backs. Then he made them sit on the chairs and he tied their feet to the legs. Then he tied their chests to the chair backs. He tied the wire too tightly to their near naked bodies and the sharp bonds cut into their skins severely hurting them. They cried out in pain, but Joey could care less. When he was certain that they could not move, he put his gun back in his belt. He and Carl sat down on the other two chairs, and began to consume the barely eaten dinners.

"Good stuff," Carl said. "I hope you fags aren't too hungry 'cause there ain't gonna be anything left."

"It's nice to have company for dinner, though, don't you think, Carl?" Joey asked.

"Oh definitely, Brother Joey, especially such good looking fags. I'll bet they would just love to suck our cocks."

"You bet wrong, punk." Kyle finally found his voice. Carl would have pistol whipped Kyle if his gun was handy. Instead he slapped him across his face.

"Why don't you take what you want and get out of here?" Andrew asked.

"Uh, uh," Joey said. "We have to lay low for a few days, and this place couldn't be more ideal. Now we don't care one way or the other if you live or die, but I'll bet you do. Cooperate and do as we say, and you won't get hurt. Give us trouble and you're goners. Get it?"

Kyle and Andrew nodded, but said nothing more.

When they were finished eating, the twins threw the dirty dishes in the sink. They obviously had no intention of cleaning up.

"Sorry we interrupted your dinner, guys. How would you like some dessert?" Joey asked. He unzipped his fly and removed his flaccid cock. He stroked it a bit and it began to stiffen. When Carl saw what his brother was doing he did the same. Joey took his gun in his hand and stood in front of Kyle. He placed the gun in Kyle's ear.

"Suck my cock, fag, and no funny business. Hurt me and you're dead. Do right by me and you live, for the time being anyway." Joey put his dick on Kyle's lips. He was uncircumcised and probably hadn't showered in days. His penis had a terrible odor and as he got harder, his head became exposed and it was full of a cheesy substance. Kyle was revolted and almost gagged. He turned his head away, but Joey thrust the gun harder into Kyle's ear, and so Kyle opened his mouth and allowed the filthy cock in. Kyle reasoned that the best way to get it over with quickly would be to give Joey a blow job to remember, and get him off fast.

When Andrew saw Joey's unwashed cock, he almost vomited and steeled himself for the worst. He was shocked when Carl put his cock to his lips. It smelled rather sweet and there was no cheese. The twins had filled up the car with gas about a half hour before happening upon the cottage. Carl was so frightened at what they had done that he had been sweating profusely.

He used the rest room and took the opportunity to cleanse himself and that included his cock and balls.

Kyle was using every trick in the book to bring Joey to orgasm, but every time he was close, Joey withdrew. He had different ideas. He wanted it to last as long as possible. When Kyle's mouth was free, he said to Joey, "If you release my hands, I could play with your balls and you would enjoy it more."

"Fat chance, sucker," Joey said. Secretly he thought that it would be a good idea. These fags were enjoying the sex and were apt to be cooperative, but he couldn't take the chance.

Andrew decided that he wasn't going to give Carl any pleasure at all. He wasn't rough, but he didn't use his tongue at all, and he let his teeth touch Carl's cock. He rationed how much his teeth scraped Carl's cock so that it wouldn't get too annoying. While he was sucking, the ugly thought that he might also get raped occurred to him, and he shuddered. *We've got to get out of this some way,* he thought.

They could delay as long as possible, but sooner or later, the twins both came. Kyle and Andrew spit out the offensive fluid. The twins didn't much care about that as long as they had gotten their rocks off. "What now?" Carl asked Joey.

"I think we should get some sleep. Help me."

He took Andrew's prison chair and dragged it to one end of the kitchen. Then he tried to drag Kyle's chair to the other end. Kyle was just too heavy and it took both of them to do it. Kyle and Andrew were now at opposite ends of the room.

"I'm a very light sleeper," Joey lied. "If you try to drag your chairs together, I'll hear you and you're dead. So just sleep the best you can in those damned chairs. Carl and Joey shut the kitchen lights, and went into the bedroom. They lay down on Kyle's bed fully clothed. The events of the day had totally exhausted them, and in minutes they fell into a deep sleep. Joey slept dreamlessly, but Carl kept dreaming that Sam found them, and he tossed and turned restlessly all night.

Only when Kyle and Andrew could hear the twins snoring lightly did they dare speak. Moonlight was shining into the room and illuminating the kitchen table.

"Look at the table," Andrew said in a stage whisper. The twins had thrown the dishes in the sink, but the cutlery was still on the table. Two steak knives were gleaming in the moonlight.

"We need to get those knives," Kyle said. "I've already wiggled my way about a foot toward the table."

"I've got you beat," Andrew informed Kyle. "I've already moved about two feet."

It only took about a half hour and they had wiggled both the chairs to the table. "If I face the table," Andrew said, "I might be able to lean forward and get one knife with my teeth." Unfortunately, he was bound too tightly and couldn't bend enough to accomplish his purpose.

"I've got an idea," Kyle said. He maneuvered his chair so that he was back to back with Andrew. Then he started to lean backwards. The chair was no match for Kyle's weight and it began to tip. It struck Andrew's chair, which started to tip toward the table. Andrew was able to scoop up one knife with his teeth. He pushed back and when Kyle felt him pushing, he sat his chair up straight. Once again, Kyle wiggled his chair to where their faces were close and Andrew passed the knife to Kyle's mouth. Kyle dropped it on his lap. Then they repeated the procedure and snatched the second knife. This time Andrew dropped it on his lap.

"Can you get to the living room?" Kyle asked.

"I'll try."

"Work your way to the sofa and we'll hide the knives between the cushions and the arm rest."

Fortunately, the entire cottage floor was covered with linoleum and the chairs wiggled easily across the smooth surface. Using the tilting procedure they had developed, they were able to hide the knives between the sofa cushions and arm rests, one on each side. They worked their way back to the kitchen and resumed their positions. They both prayed that Carl and Joey would not miss the steak knives. All of this had taken about three hours and they were exhausted. No matter, sleep was almost impossible. Neither got much sleep except for dozing off a couple of times for a few precious seconds.

Kyle was the first to hear the twins moving about. He heard them get out of bed and go to the bathroom to pee. He heard nothing, which sounded like maybe they brushed their teeth. He heard at least one of them shit.

They came out of the bedroom completely naked but with guns in hand. "We're going to loosen your bonds," Joey informed them, "except for the ones around your wrists. Then we are going to fuck you fags one at a time, and we would suggest no resistance. Remember, we still have guns on you."

They unknotted the fish wire and carefully coiled it into a circle. Kyle and Andrew breathed a sigh of relief. The twins pulled Kyle's and Andrew's underwear down, and ordered them into the bedroom.

Kyle expected that they would fuck him doggie style because his wrists were tied behind him. He was surprised that the twins lay down on their backs, and with guns waving, they instructed Andrew and Kyle to straddle them and lower themselves on to their waiting cocks.

Andrew nodded toward the jar of Vaseline that was still on the night table. "Could you at least use some lube?" he asked. He would have asked for condoms but there was none available and he doubted the twins had any. Even if they had some they would never use them.

"Sure," Joey said, "anything for our bitches." Carl reached over for the jar and they both lubed their cocks generously. Then Andrew got on the bed first, straddled Carl and sat down on him. Carl had to guide his cock in. When Andrew was settled, Kyle did the same with Joey.

When he was sure that Joey was relaxed and enjoying the experience, Kyle decided to use the "gay card."

"Come on Joey. You know you can trust us. If we had our hands free, just think of the pleasures we could give you guys. The possibilities are endless."

"That's very tempting, but I have to think about it. Maybe later."

When Kyle lowered himself onto Joey's cock, his own rod was staring Joey in the face. As disgusted as he was at being raped, Kyle was still a gay young man, and as Joey's rod began to rub against his prostate, he began to erect.

"My God," Joey gasped. "That's the biggest cock I have ever seen, and I saw some monsters in prison. I gotta have that in me. When we're done, I want you to fuck me, Kyle baby."

Kyle didn't answer. He was too busy pumping up and down. Joey had the gun pointed at him and he wanted to keep him happy. Finally, Joey came, bucking and screaming. Kyle decided on a calculated risk. Before lifting himself off Joey, he leaned over and began to French kiss him. Joey was surprised but he started to kiss Kyle back. "Let me fuck you now," Kyle whispered.

"You bet," Joey responded.

"Please release my wrists," Kyle begged, "so I can do it right."

"You win, but remember the gun is loaded."

"I don't give a shit about the gun," Kyle purred. "All I care about is that I'm going to fuck you."

This is just like prison, Joey thought. *The bitches are beginning to enjoy it.* He undid Kyle's final bonds.

It took hard work and lots of lube, but Kyle, who was flat on his back, was able to finally enter Joey as Joey lowered himself on Kyle's massive member. Joey kept leaning over and kissing Kyle with wet slobbery kisses. Kyle's newly freed hands fondled Joey's balls and stroked his cock. Kyle's cock was massaging Joey's prostate and the two men came together squealing like pigs. Joey leaned over and kissed Kyle long and sensuously.

For just a few moments at the beginning, Andrew thought that Kyle was enjoying himself, and he wondered what kind of man he had fallen in love with. But when Joey removed the binding from Kyle's wrists, it didn't take long for him to realize that Kyle was playing a game. He quickly joined in as Kyle's team mate, and he began to give Carl the same loving treatment. Carl even undid Andrew's bound wrists. The love making was torrid and the twins were beginning to enjoy themselves. Up until now, they had only had each other. It was actually a new and exciting experience to be with other men. As for Kyle and Andrew, they were doing their best to convince the twins that they were enjoying themselves also, but all they were thinking about was a scheme to find a way to get to the knives, especially now that they were unbound.

When all four of them were exhausted, they lay in a heap on the bed. Andrew leaned over and kissed Joey. Kyle leaned over and kissed Carl. The twins kissed each other and Andrew and Kyle kissed each other. It was no different than the action at the end of a porno sequence. They were just four young queers enjoying a foursome.

Kyle suggested that they all shower. Even the twins thought it was a good idea. "I'll go first," Kyle said. Then I can prepare breakfast while the rest of you shower."

"Nice try, handsome," Joey said, "but I'll go first. I'm not leaving you alone in the kitchen."

Kyle shook his head sadly. So you still don't trust me," he said, sounding terribly hurt.

Joey showered first. He gave instructions to Carl not to take his gun off Kyle and Andrew for a second. When he was done, Joey allowed Kyle to shower next. After his shower, Kyle made bacon, eggs and toast for breakfast and put up a pot of coffee. As they were eating breakfast, the twins, especially Joey, did indeed seem to relax somewhat. Kyle felt the less tense atmosphere and ventured to ask, "What are you two good looking dudes on the lam from? I'll bet it's from your adoring fans." He broke out laughing.

Joey looked like he was about to tell all, but he changed his mind. "That's for us to know and for you to wonder about," he said rather smugly. Then as if to change the subject he said to Kyle, "I never seen a cock as big as yours. I'm going to suck on it later." Carl looked hurt. "Me too," he muttered.

"I think it's cool, twin brothers having sex together," Kyle lied with a twinkle in his eye. "When did it all begin?" He was trying to distract the twins just enough so that he could get to the knives hidden in the sofa, without arousing their suspicions.

"In prison," Carl said. "We never knew how good it was until then."

"I figured," Kyle said. "Why don't one of you, or both of you, sit on the sofa with me and you can suck my mammoth fucking tool?"

The twins smiled at each other and headed for the sofa. Joey waved his gun at Kyle as if to say, "What are you waiting for? You're the star of this movie." He looked at Andrew and said, "You can come and watch, but you better stay within my range of vision."

Kyle sat on the sofa between the twins, and Andrew sat on the floor facing them. Joey leaned over and opened wide so he could get Kyle's cock into him. He managed to get a couple of inches in, and as he did so, Kyle's hand reached between the pillow and the arm of the sofa. He could feel one of the knives. His hand closed around the hilt as his eyes found Andrew's and he nodded slightly at his lover.

Andrew sidled up to the couch and said to Carl, "Please let me suck your cock." Carl smiled and spread his legs.

"Sure bitch," he said. Andrew went down on him and his hand found the other knife at the other end of the sofa. He closed his fist on it.

Suddenly the phone rang shrilly and all four men jumped. Kyle and Andrew released their holds on the knives. Joey put a gun to Andrew's head. "Answer it," he told Kyle, "and watch your P's and Q's if you don't want to go to your boyfriend's funeral."

Kyle got up and walked to the phone. He picked up the receiver and said, "Hello... No, this is Kyle Farrell from across the lake. Mr. Stanley is right here." He handed the phone to Andrew and was rewarded with a gun to his head for his efforts.

"Hello, this is Andrew Stanley...I sure do appreciate your concern and checking on me like this...I know I said I'd be back this morning, but you see, we got some unexpected company, two old friends of Mr. Farrell, so it looks like we'll be hanging out here a while longer...No I can't say when I'll get back. Would you do me a favor? If anyone from my office calls, would you please tell them that I'm having a wonderful time even though I didn't expect to. And if they don't believe you, you can tell them to tell it to the marines. Yes, the marines…. Thanks again for being concerned."

Andrew took a very calculated risk. He hoped James Harper, the desk clerk, was old enough to remember that the expression "tell it to the marines" meant that everything he said was hogwash. But more than that, he hoped the twins had never heard the expression in their lives. From the lack of response from them, he assumed that they were not in this particular loop.

James Harper hung up the phone utterly confused. He knew that Andrew had indicated that he was lying to him. But what about? Was it a signal? James was sure it was. He wanted to call the police, but didn't know what to tell them. He guessed he could ask them just to stop by Mr. Farrell's residence and make sure everything was all right. *Yes,* he thought, *I'll do that. I'd feel awful if something was wrong and I didn't do anything about it.*

He reached for the phone, but just then, two well-dressed gentlemen came into the lobby. James wasn't expecting anyone and he didn't know these men so he was quite surprised.

"Hello," the first one said and extended his hand to James. The second man took out a picture, and flashed it at James.

"Have you ever seen these men?" he asked. "They're easy enough to spot. They're identical twins."

"Can't say as I have. Are they wanted for anything?"

"Nothing serious. Just a major case of fraud."

James had never missed one episode of 'Murder She Wrote.' In his mind, he could hear Andrew say that they got **two** unexpected visitors. He had met and spoken to Kyle when he first bought the cottage, and he knew that Kyle came here for seclusion and wouldn't be expecting any visitors. Occasionally, a boat from the lodge happened on his cottage. Kyle would politely load the boat onto a rack on his car and bring the guest and boat back to the lodge. He figured that was what happened to Andrew, but this time Kyle did not bring the guest back, and the guest said you could tell his story to the marines, meaning he was lying. He was just suspicious enough to feel that Angela Lansbury was trying to tell him something.

"Listen gentlemen," he said in his best conspiratorial tone of voice. He leaned toward them, and barely above a whisper, he told them everything he suspected about the two unexpected visitors, and Andrew's instructions to tell it to the marines. "I may be all wet, but I was just about to call the police when you gentlemen came in. I figured it wouldn't hurt if they looked in on Dr. Farrell and made sure that all was well."

"Very wise," the second gentleman said, "but don't bother to call the police. We're private detectives. We'll check out the cottage and if the unexpected visitors are our guys, we'll kill two birds with one stone. Now how do we get to this cottage?"

James gave them detailed directions, and as the men thanked him, he said, "Don't forget to let me know the outcome."

When the two gentlemen left the lodge, they checked in with Sam. "We have a good lead," Number One told the boss. "We stopped at a gas station a while ago. It was on a secondary road at the corner of a real dirt back road. We showed the attendant the pictures of the twins and he said that they had filled up there about an hour earlier. He said that one of them looked real sick, and he had to use the rest room. There was a lodge further up the back road that was really secluded so we checked there also. From what we learned, we have reason to believe that they are holding two men captive in a very remote and isolated cabin across the lake from the lodge. The cabin is owned by a college professor named Kyle Farrell, and the other guy is staying at The Waterfall Lodge. He must have gone over to visit Farrell. He's a New York lawyer, named Andrew Stanley."

"Oh my God," Sam yelled, "Listen to me. You do everything you can to keep the two victims safe, especially Andrew. Don't let anything happen to them."

"Don't worry boss. We'll see to it."

Sam hung up. He was angrier than ever at the twins who had betrayed him. But worse, he had a dreadful fear that Joey and Carl had harmed Andrew.

CHAPTER FOUR

The phone call from the lodge had jangled Joey's nerves. He had begun to trust Andrew and Kyle a little bit, but all that vanished with the first ring of the telephone. He trained his gun on them, and instructed Carl to bind them up again. Andrew and Kyle resigned themselves to the inevitable.

"Could we at least go to the bathroom first, and could you at least let us sit on the sofa? Those kitchen chairs are impossibly hard and uncomfortable."

"Why not?" Joey said. "You guys have been pretty decent to us." Kyle went to the bathroom first and shit and pissed. Andrew then did the same. When they were done, Carl bound their wrists behind them, and after they were seated on the sofa, he coiled the wire around their legs, starting at their thighs and working down to their ankles. The twins were pretty satisfied that their captives were immobile. If only they knew that both of them could feel the knives right at their fingertips, just where they had so recently actually held them. They sat as far apart from each other as possible to further hide the weapons.

"How much longer are you guys staying?" Andrew asked. Joey just scowled.

"What I was thinking is that if you stay in any one place too long, whoever is chasing you has a better chance of catching up to you."

Carl looked at Joey with panic in his eyes. Andrew was right of course.

"Maybe we should leave as soon as it gets dark," Carl said to Joey. "There's plenty of food here we can take."

"Let me think about it," Joey said. He knew that Andrew was right. "In the meantime, let's have some fun. They were all still naked and Joey approached Andrew. So far it had always been him and Kyle and he wanted a little bit of Andrew too.

"Lean forward," he said to Andrew and take my tasty prick into your mouth. At least it was clean now and Andrew began to suck it intending to give Joey pleasure. It was an involuntary reaction. Andrew had heard that captives often fell in love with their captors and he wondered if it was happening to him. From the get go, he never felt that the twins were hardened criminals. He certainly hoped that they weren't murderers.

In the meantime, Carl was raping Kyle's mouth, and the twins were too lost in rapture to know what was going on outside the cottage.

"Are you going to do us?" Andrew asked when he came up for air. "It's not fair to work us up like this and not offer relief." Joey laughed and he tousled Andrew's hair in a rare show of affection.

The two gentlemen had no trouble finding the cottage with Harper's detailed directions. They parked their late model, black Chevy sedan about a hundred yards from the cabin, drew their guns, and walked stealthily toward it. The first thing they saw was the Plymouth. The key was in the ignition, and the license plate matched the car they were looking for. They smiled at each other. They had their men.

One of the gentlemen held his palm on the trunk as the other popped it, enabling them to open the trunk slowly without making any noise. There lay the briefcase with the money. They removed it and did not shut the trunk again. One of them ran the case back to their Chevy and secured it in a secret compartment under the trunk. Then he rejoined his companion. They crept up to the cabin and looked in through the nearest window into the kitchen.

The room was empty, but through the kitchen they could see into the living room. The living room was occupied, but they couldn't make out what was going on.

Number One said, "I don't think we should let Farrell and Stanley see our faces."

"You're right," Number Two said. They both tied handkerchiefs around their faces and then they went around to the back of the house. They saw the sliding glass patio doors and looked in. They were both angry and disgusted. Two young men were bound hand and foot with some sort of wire and were being forced to give head to those two low lives. They were also aware that at least one of the young men was under Gardini's protection. Number one knew that the boss was going to be very angry at the abuse that this young man was suffering.

They gingerly tested the sliding doors. They were unlocked. They slid the doors open so quickly and entered so suddenly that they took the twins totally by surprise. They disarmed them at a dizzying speed. Gentleman Number One held a gun on them, and Number Two unbound Kyle and Andrew. Carl was sniveling and Joey was smiling evilly.

As soon as they were free, Number Two told Kyle and Andrew to go get dressed. They ran into the bedroom without asking any questions. Number two used the wire to bind the twins' wrists behind their backs, just as they had done to their captives.

By the time Kyle and Andrew were dressed, and they returned to the living room to thank their liberators, the place was deserted. They looked outside. Even the Plymouth was gone. Kyle and Andrew looked at each other in amazement. These guys were as fast as superman. Even as they were admiring the speed with which these guys worked, two bodies were being locked in a Plymouth, and the Plymouth was being pushed to the bottom of the lake.

Kyle looked around and the only evidence that remained of their visitors was the clothing they had worn when they invaded the house. Some very savvy instinct told them that they should get rid of the clothing as soon as possible. But first they examined the contents. The tee shirts had no pockets and could not contain anything. The briefs, of course, could harbor nothing. The first

pair of trousers had some change in a pocket, a switchblade and a wallet.
There was a five dollar bill in the wallet, and a driver's license belonging to
Carl Barkin. The address was on the lower east side of Manhattan. The other
pair of trousers had only a switchblade and a wallet. Inside the wallet was a
driver's license belonging to Joseph Barkin, same address. There was also
a slip of paper from a note pad on which someone had written directions to
an address in Englewood, NJ. That meant nothing to Andrew, but when he
saw the engraving at the top of the note paper, he turned ashen white and
froze in his place.

"What's the matter?" Kyle asked concerned.

Andrew pointed to the name on the note pad.

Samuel A. Gardini

"Do you know him?" Kyle asked.

"Yes. Everyone in New York knows his name. He runs a slew of legitimate
businesses, and my firm represents all of them. However, nobody doubts
that he makes his millions, in shall we say, less than honest businesses. But
it can't be proven, and he has the police on his payroll anyway. I'm the one
who actually brought him into the firm. His nephew, Freddie, is gay and
owns a restaurant. He's a friend of mine and he's my client too. Through
Freddie, I've known Sam since I was six years old. Christ, the man treats me
like he was Santa Claus. I adore him. He's like an uncle to me too. We have
a great relationship. What do I do now? His goons must have our names."

"They had every opportunity to evaporate us, and they didn't. We were
innocent victims, and Santa Claus doesn't kill innocent victims. Let's not do
anything. Gardini does not know that we have this piece of paper, and we
never saw the faces of the guys who set us free. We are a non-issue to him.
Let's destroy the paper, the clothes and whatever we found in the clothes.
Then let's return the boat and check you out of the lodge. You're spending
the rest of your vacation with me, only from now on we lock the doors and
windows." That got them both laughing for the first time since their home
invasion.

They buried all traces of the Barkin twins, including the note with Sam's name on it, under a tree near the lake. The soil was sandiest near the lake and it was the easiest spot to dig the hole.

When they arrived at the lodge, Kyle drove as close to the lake as possible and they returned the boat to the water. Then they went into the lobby. It was late in the day and James was just leaving.

"Boy, am I glad to see you. I got your message that everything you said was bullshit, Mr. Stanley, so when those guys came in looking for two criminals, I told them I was suspicious, and sent them to check out the cabin."

"So my coded message worked." Andrew said gleefully. "I can't thank you enough, Mr. Harper, but it was all a false alarm," he lied. "Those 'visitors' came in to ask for directions, but they were acting suspiciously, and so I suspected the worst. In the end, they just left us, and when those two gentlemen came around, we sent them on their way also."

"I guess I've seen too many mystery movies," James laughed. "Well, I'm off for the evening. I'll see you in the morning, guys. Good night."

Kyle and Andrew went to Andrew's room to pack. "Nice room, great view," Kyle said when they were in the room.

"I have an idea," Andrew said. "It's past 2 PM so the room is paid for the night. Let's have dinner here at the lodge and sleep over. I can check out after breakfast tomorrow."

"Great idea! We'll make love in a hotel and it will feel like a honeymoon," Kyle said as he grabbed Andrew in a bear hug."

"Just one thing," Andrew said. "I feel dirty from those two animals. I want to shower before dinner."

"Let's shower together," Kyle said.

The shower was barely big enough for the two of them. They pushed hard against each other. Unfortunately, their cocks could not quite rub together because Kyle was so much taller. They had no trouble washing each other's backs and cleaning their ass holes thoroughly. It was more difficult scrubbing their fronts and their cocks and balls, but they managed amidst much laughing and giggling.

When they left the shower they started grabbing at each other, but in the end, they decided to wait for love until after dinner. That way they could go slow and make love all night without interruption. They felt that they had been interrupted enough.

Andrew put on fresh clothing, but Kyle had to wear what he came in with. He hated to wear previously worn underwear after a shower, and since Andrew's briefs were way too small for him, he decided not to wear any underwear at all.

They were just leaving the room when the telephone rang. "I wonder who that can be." Andrew mused as he went to pick up the receiver.

Sam Gardini was briefed by his two henchmen as they were driving back to Manhattan. He was satisfied that the only way Andrew could link him to the twins was if they had said something to him. He doubted it very much but he had to find out. He decided to call Andrew on a ruse and see how the young man reacted. He hoped that Andrew suspected nothing. He was so fond of him he didn't want to have to harm him. He already knew the telephone number at The Waterfall Lodge. He also had the address. He intended to send James Harper an anonymous gift. But to make it look legitimate, he called Andrew's secretary who was glad to give Mr. Gardini, their best client, the number of the lodge.

Andrew picked up the receiver. "Hello!" he said.

"Andrew, my boy," a jolly voice chirped out, "it's Sam." Andrew's stomach churned. He had to remind himself that Sam had no way of knowing that he could connect him to his recent ordeal.

"Uncle Sam, it's so nice to hear from you. To what do I owe the pleasure?"

"I got your number from your secretary, and I promise not to disturb you on your vacation again, but I have a question."

"Sure, shoot away." Andrew could not stop shaking and he prayed that it wasn't evident in his voice.

"I was just wondering if you filed the foreclosure papers on that delinquent skunk who's renting the warehouse I own in Brooklyn."

"Oh sure, Sam. It was the last thing I did before I left."

"Good, I'm so relieved. So tell me son, how are you enjoying your first vacation in years?" Andrew grew wary. He knew that Sam knew everything that had transpired so he couldn't lie.

Andrew weighed his words carefully. "Well Sam, I have good news and bad news. Which do you want to hear first?"

"The good news, I think," Sam came back at him, with a slight laugh.

Sam was fully aware that Andrew was gay. It made no difference to him. Andrew's friend, Sam's gay nephew, Freddie, was his only living relative, and he would do anything for the boy. Without hesitating Andrew said, "The good news is that I ran into my college roommate's brother. He owns a cabin up here, where he comes to get away from it all. So tomorrow morning, I'm checking out of the lodge and I'm going to spend the rest of my stay with Kyle. We're at the lodge now, and were getting ready for dinner."

"You like this boy?" Sam asked. You could hear the smile in his voice.

"Yes Sam, I like him very much, but here's the bad news."

"I was spending the day yesterday at Kyle's cabin. We had just sat down to dinner when two criminals forced their way in. They made us strip and they tied us up with fishing wire. We could only watch as they ate our dinner. Please forgive me, if I skip telling you what else they made us do. I can only say that it's a good thing we are gay. If they forced straight men to do what we were forced to do, it could very well have driven them insane.

"I had informed the lodge that I would be spending the night at Kyle's cabin and that I would return to the lodge in the morning. When I failed to come back, they grew concerned and called to check on me. I told the desk clerk that I was fine and he could tell that to the marines. The goons had no idea what I was hinting at, but the desk clerk knew that I was signaling him that I was telling a lie. That man deserves a medal for checking up on me in the first place, and then picking up on my signal."

Sam interrupted. "I knew I had a smart lawyer."

"Anyway, the desk clerk was just about to call the police when two cops, or private eyes, or whatever, walked in. They showed him a picture of the two men they were after for having pulled some sort of fraud. Mr. Harper said that he hadn't seen these guys, but he was very suspicious at what might be going on at Kyle's cabin, based on what I had told him in my own made up code. He gave the two men directions to the cabin. We were still tied up when they burst in and disarmed the scum who were continuing to abuse us in more ways than I can tell you about. Kyle and I showered for hours to cleanse off the dirt those scum left on us," he exaggerated a bit.

"My poor boy," Sam lamented. He knew full well what Andrew meant, and he was angrier at Carl and Joey than he was before. He didn't think he could get any angrier.

"The cops told us to go into the bedroom to dress and when we went back into the living room, the cops, the goons and their car were gone. The cops weren't locals. They covered their faces, and I don't know how to reach them. I have no idea what the criminals were wanted for, or who they were. I sure would like to thank the policemen."

"They were doing their jobs, Andrew. I'm sure they know how much you appreciate what they did. Now you are sure everything is all right and you will be able to enjoy the rest of your vacation."

"Yes sir," I'm positive. "Kyle is going to make sure of it."

"Good. Then enjoy yourself and I'll see you when you get home."

"Thanks for calling and for your concern Uncle Sam. Yes, I'll see you when I get back."

Sam was relieved. He didn't think the twins had mentioned his name. Why would they?

Andrew replaced the receiver in its cradle. He was shaking like an aspen in the wind. Kyle put his arms around him and ran his hand up and down Andrew's back to comfort him.

"I think we are very safe now," Kyle said. "You seem to have a guardian angel."

Kyle and Andrew were very anxious to make love to each other, but they didn't rush dinner. They had all the time in the world, so they ate slowly, savoring every tasty bite of the filet mignon steaks they ordered to replace the steaks that had been snatched from them the night before. The honeymoon couple, the spinsters and the recent widower were all in the dining room. The widower was dining with the two ladies. The honeymoon couple was unaware that anyone else was in the dining room, and Kyle and Andrew smiled at their near state of oblivion.

"Do you think that people can see how in love we are like those two over there?" Kyle asked.

"Maybe, but who cares one way or the other. I'm sure not going to hide it." Andrew answered.

After dinner, they took a stroll down to the lake. It was a lot warmer this evening. At last, it felt like summer might actually reach this mountain retreat sometime soon. As they strolled leisurely, they held each other's hands.

"Mike spoke of you all the time," Kyle said. "He thinks you are a super guy. I think I fell in love with you before we met."

"That is so strange," Andrew commented. "I like Mike, but we hardly ever spoke. We barely grunted at each other when we saw each other."

"Obviously he liked you more than you thought. He suspected you were gay. Maybe he was afraid to get too close to you, thinking you might come on to him."

"You don't know how close to the truth that is," Andrew lamented. "You can see how much will power I have."

"I can't wait to tell him that we have met and fallen in love. It will knock him for a loop," Kyle actually giggled.

"Yes, can we call him tomorrow? What a hoot it'll be when we tell him."

Finally they went back to Andrew's room. They made love through most of the night and got very little sleep. Now for the first time, they had time to explore the mysteries of their bodies. Their tongues invaded every square inch of the other. Every opening in their bodies was explored. No patch of skin was left unswathed. From the long moans and sighs that they each emitted, it was obvious what great pleasure they were giving each other. They were neither expecting nor looking for a climax. They would have preferred the night to last forever. Unfortunately, an orgasm usually signaled an end to it all. But youth and libido could not be denied forever, and eventually they both gave in to Mother Nature and came. Andrew came in Kyle's mouth and Kyle came in Andrew's ass. Both of them tried unsuccessfully to stifle the screech of pleasure, which accompanied their climaxes. They finally fell asleep at 4:30 in the morning. Before sleep came to them, Kyle whispered in Andrew's ear, "Do you think we set a new world record tonight?"

When they awoke, it was too late to have breakfast at the lodge.

"No matter, Andy" Kyle said, "I'll make breakfast *at our place.*"

Andrew could not believe that Kyle said, *"Our place."* He decided not to comment on it for the moment. They dressed, packed and loaded Andrew's gear into Kyle's car. Andrew checked out, and James told him how disappointed he was to see him leave prematurely, but he winked at Kyle and said that he understood. At that moment, Andrew wondered if James might not be gay. He looked at Kyle, who gave him a slight nod indicating that he felt the same way. Andrew followed Kyle to the cabin in his car.

When Andrew was hanging up his clothes in Kyle's closet, his emotions got the better of him. Remembering how close they came to having been murdered, he started to blubber and he wrapped his arms around Kyle. Kyle remained silent but he kept hugging Andrew until he calmed down and resumed unpacking. Once Andrew was settled in, Kyle began to make breakfast. They sat down to a meal of scrambled eggs, toast and coffee.

"What do you say we go out tonight and celebrate?" Kyle asked Andrew. "There's a nice little restaurant in the next town."

"That sounds wonderful," Andrew replied enthusiastically.

"As soon as breakfast is over, let's call Mike. I can't wait to share my happiness with my little brother."

Andrew started to laugh. "I'd hardly call him little. But before we call him, I'd better call my office, and give them your number here, since I can't be reached on my cell phone."

"Sure go right ahead, honey," Kyle said. Andrew loved that Kyle addressed him so endearingly.

Andrew reached his secretary and gave her Kyle's telephone number. She immediately got curious and wanted to know what that was all about. "I'll explain when I get home." Andrew told her.

"I hope you don't mind that I gave Mr. Gardini your number at the lodge," she said. "I just figured that since he's your biggest client it would be OK."

"It was perfectly all right, and if he needs to reach me again, please give him Kyle's number. We can't get cell phone reception here. The place is so isolated"

"That sounds wonderful. Do you think I could borrow it sometime? Maybe it would put a little fire back in my husband's underwear," Maggie said.

Andrew laughed dutifully. They said goodbye and Andrew handed the phone to Kyle.

"Let's call Mike now," Andrew said.

Pre-season training had not yet begun and Kyle knew that Mike would be enjoying his family at his home in Manhasset, NY so he took a chance and called him on his land phone. The maid answered on the third ring. "Farrell residence." She sang it, and it almost sounded like a pre-recorded song.

"Hi Jenny," Kyle said cordially. "Is my big oaf of a little brother at home?"

"Oh Dr. Farrell," Jenny cooed. "It's so nice to hear your voice. Yes, he's at the pool. I'll get him for you." Jenny put down the phone and went out to the back yard. Mike was sunning on a lounge chair. He was alone. The children were in day care, and his wife was out shopping.

"Your brother is on the phone," she announced.

There was a phone on a table right next to Mike's lounge. "I'll take it here," he said and Jenny went back to hang up the hall phone.

"Hey Bro, what's up?" Mike asked.

"My dick, kiddo. What's up with you?"

"Nothing at the moment, but I intend to remedy that later today. Do you have a purpose to this call or do you just want to pick on your little brother like you always do?"

"I've got a purpose, a big one," Kyle answered. "I hope you are sitting down. You'll never guess who I met accidently the other day. Guess."

"That's the stupidest thing I ever heard. If I won't be able to guess, why ask me?'

Oblivious to Mike's reply, Kyle continued. "I ran into Andrew Stanley, your college roommate."

"You're fucking kidding. How's he doing?"

He's doing great. He's a big shot corporate attorney in New York. He probably makes ten times what I do, and one one hundredth of what you make. Why didn't you ever tell me how good looking, sexy, sweet, charming, magnificent, well hung, and desirable he was? I could go on, but I'm running out of adjectives."

"I did try to tell you, but there was never an opportunity to introduce you two dudes. I got a feeling something is going on here. Is he around? Let me talk to him." Kyle handed the phone to Andrew. He was beaming. Andrew had not yet seen him this happy.

"Hi Mike," Andrew said.

"Mr. Stanley," Mike said in his most formal manner. "So you are gay, you son of a gun. I was afraid to ask you. I wanted so much to fix you up with my brother, but I wasn't sure."

"I suppose you can't outfox fate. It happened in spite of you. Anyway, because you were so timid, Kyle and I wasted too many years, but it was worth the wait. Anyway, better late than never, and I have to forgive you, because you are going to be my brother in law."

"Holy shit!" Mike kept yelling over and over. "So when are you two guys going to move in together?" Andrew suddenly got doused with ice cold water. He and Kyle hadn't even discussed that. They lived in separate cities. How were they ever to resolve that dilemma? He couldn't answer Mike.

After some length of silence, Andrew heard Mike ask, "Andrew, are you there?"

"Yes Mike, but we haven't gotten that far yet."

"Well work on it. You live in The City and I live in the burbs. For too many years, I've been trying to get Kyle to teach somewhere in the metropolitan area so that we can be together again. I'm passing the ball to you. Work on it." Mike repeated.

"You can bet on it," Andrew assured him. After all these years, he still didn't have much to say to Mike, so he handed the phone back to Kyle. He was bewildered at how easily he could communicate with Kyle, and he could never find anything that he and Mike could talk about. He hoped that would all change someday; maybe at a family dinner or at Christmas or something.

"What are you asking Andy to do, that he told you that you could bet on it?" Kyle asked Mike.

"First of all, it's none of your fucking business," Mike laughed, "and second of all, if I remember correctly, he hates to be called Andy." That was news to Kyle. Andrew had never corrected him.

"I think I'd better say goodbye now before I say something I'll regret," Kyle warned Mike. "Now here's something I can say that I'll never be sorry for: I love you, Bro. Say hello to Charlene, and kiss the kids for me. Ciao."

"I love you too. This is an incredible thing that happened. It's like it was preordained, so I know you guys will be incredibly happy, Ciao, Bro." Kyle hung up the phone and smiled at Andrew who was looking totally serious.

"Why didn't you tell me that you hate being called Andy?"

"Generally I do hate it, and I correct people, but when you called me Andy, it sounded like a whole chorus of angels singing to me. Please keep calling me Andy, Kyle. Somehow it's different coming from you."

"Then why do you look so glum?" Kyle asked.

"Mike wanted to know when we were moving in together, and it was like I got hit in the face with a wet towel. I've been so happy; I hadn't given it any thought. We live close enough for weekend visits, but that's not good enough. I need to be with you. If you feel the same way, one of us has to switch jobs." Andrew looked at Kyle with trepidation.

"I know. Mike has been after me to look for a position in the New York area for ages. I miss him and the kids a lot too. I've thought about it often, but I've been sitting on my lazy butt. The thing of it is that one of my professors at U of B has been head of the English Department at CCNY for the past three years, and he has been trying to recruit me since he took the position. I never said 'no.' I just kept telling him that I wasn't ready yet."

"Would you be willing to accept the position?"

"Absolutely, I have a reason to be in New York now. I certainly can't expect you to dump your clients and a potential partnership to move to some small firm in Albany or even to hang out your own shingle. I am worried about one thing though. Are you going to continue to work 24/7?"

"Like you just said, I have a reason to change my ways now. Besides I'll have someone to come home to."

"I'll take that as a "no," Kyle said smiling. The two lovers embraced and Andrew whispered, "Wow, things are moving fast."

"Maybe faster yet," Kyle said. "I think I'll call Professor Johnson. I have his home number. By the way, you should know that Scott is gay. I came on to him in my freshman year, but he rebuffed me. He told me that he never gets involved with students. Just before I graduated, we finally made it, but it was a one night stand. I moved to New York to attend grad school and he remained in Buffalo. Then I moved to Albany and he moved to New York. We were not meant to be together."

"Should I be jealous of Scott?" Andrew really wanted to know.

"Unless he has changed drastically, he suffers from commitment phobia. He's into one night stands. Fuck 'em and leave 'em. Besides he's in his mid forties."

"Tim was 62 and I was 19 when we met, and I swear to you, we loved each other dearly. I'm never sorry or regretful of the time we had together," Andrew reminded Kyle.

"I know sweetheart. This was my way of reassuring you that you have nothing to worry about."

"Then please call him. Our future is at stake."

Kyle and Scott Johnson were still in touch with each other after all these years. They spoke to each other on the phone at least twice a month, and E-Mailed each other several times a week. Most of their conversations revolved around what young men Scott had conquered since their last conversation. If Scott wasn't lying to Kyle, his tricks were never students. He never broke his rule not to get involved with his students. After each call from Kyle, Scott thought fondly back to when they first met.

Kyle was an entering freshman at The University of Buffalo, but at nearly nineteen, he had already achieved his fully mature manhood. Scott was teaching freshman English Composition that year and Kyle was in his class. When his students were all seated, Scott wrote his name and a telephone number on the board. He encouraged his students to call him anytime if they needed him. Then he asked that the class introduce themselves, tell where they hailed from, what they were majoring in, and what they hoped to get out of his class.

Scott was a good listener. He tried to memorize each student's name as they spoke. When it came time for Kyle to speak, something came over Scott. He got a little short of breath and his whole body got clammy. He had never

had a male student as handsome, nay as beautiful, as Kyle Farrell. He was
happy to be sitting behind his desk, because he was getting a major boner.
He often reacted that way to a handsome young student, but he never broke
his rule. He never came on to a student, and if they came on to him, he told
them that he was flattered, but it was a definite NO.

"My name is Kyle Farrell and I come from Rochester, NY. I'm majoring
in English Literature with a minor in American Literature. By studying
composition with Dr. Johnson, I hope to be able to better evaluate the quality
of the literature I will be studying."

"Thank you Mr. Farrell. I hope I don't disappoint you," Scott said. "Next."

Scott was openly gay and his life style flowed easily into his lectures. It was
no different, and just as natural as a straight teacher telling his class that he
was grumpy this morning because his wife burned his breakfast toast. As
soon as Kyle realized that Scott was gay, he wanted him. Scott was in his
mid thirties, and he had a great body and handsome good looks. Kyle made
every excuse to call the number Scott had given him just to talk to him. He
would ask the dumbest questions and Scott would be secretly amused. He
knew what Kyle was all about. Kyle tried to make dinner dates with Scott
to discuss the course material, but of course, Scott always declined. During
all four years of Kyle's stay in Buffalo, he managed somehow to take a class
with Scott each semester. Even though Kyle was fucking his roommate and
whoever else he could capture, he still wanted Scott badly.

Finally, two weeks before graduation, Kyle cajoled Scott into having a
farewell dinner with him, since he was moving to New York to do post
graduate work at Columbia University. Kyle would not take no for an answer.
He used every trick in the book to cajole Scott into saying yes. Finally, Scott
rationalized. Kyle's last final exam was scheduled for next Wednesday. If
he made a date with him any time after that, he would technically not be his
student. He wouldn't even be a student at the University, so he would not be
breaking his rule should they have sex, and he had no doubt that they would.
He had no intention of fighting it. Kyle had grown even buffer since he first
came to the University, and Scott desired him more than ever.

They arranged to meet for dinner at a very fine restaurant not too far from
Scott's apartment. They both knew what was going to happen and as badly
as their groins were aching, they didn't rush dinner. They sat at right angles

to each other and felt each other up under the table during the entire meal. At Kyle's insistence, he paid the bill. It was a lovely spring evening and they leisurely strolled back to Scott's apartment. Once they were inside and locked the door, the whole mood of the evening changed. They were both so hungry for each other that they became animals, and they just about ripped each other's clothes off. Nobody felt like being leisurely now. Scott was not badly hung. One might say his circumcised prick was 'modestly' hung. When he saw the size of Kyle's manhood, he actually got frightened that Kyle might hurt him, but he quickly rationalized that Kyle was used to this situation and would know just what to do. He was right.

Kyle reached into his trousers and removed a tube of lubricant, which he placed on Scott's night table. They climbed into bed together and spent the first half hour just kissing, fondling and exploring each other's bodies. Kyle went down on Scott first, and try as he might to hold back, Scott came in generous spurts down Kyle's throat.

"Shit," Scott said, "I wanted to hold off and fuck you."

"Not a problem," Kyle said. "We have all night and all day tomorrow if you'd like. You can fuck me later." Over the next 24 hours, they did it all. They used each other to achieve the infinite of all pleasures anally and orally. At the end they were totally sated and agreed that it was well worth a four year wait.

Kyle took the phone from Andrew and dialed Scott's number. They spoke for several minutes on mostly inane stuff until finally Kyle asked if Scott still wanted him for his teaching staff.

"Of course, I still want you, you fuck. I am so shorthanded that I am teaching three fucking courses myself. Believe me when I tell you that I don't want to do that fucking job. I even have to teach two fucking summer courses, starting June 23. I have no one else to do it. How soon can you get the fuck down here?"

"Scotty, your language is atrocious for the head of the English department. You really should practice some restraint."

"I know, I know," Scott said, "but whenever I get happy and excited like I am right now, I begin to talk like that. It's an involuntary thing."

"So I take it that you are happy and excited about hiring me."

"About that, of course, but also about shoving my dick down your throat."

"Ain't gonna happen, boss. I'm married to a lawyer. He'll take my intestines out if I cheat on him," Kyle said with a certain amount of smugness.

"Fuck, Kyle. Why the hell did you have to go and get married on me?"

"It's the reason that I'm moving to New York; so that we can be together."

"Well, no matter, I still want you in my department. Nothing changes the fact that you are....were the best student I ever had. Let me know when you have an ETA. I still love you, you fuck."

After he hung up, Kyle captured Andrew in a bear hug, and forgetting his size and strength, he came close to cracking some of Andrew's ribs.

"Geez, I'm sorry, honey," he said. "I have two E Mails to send off, and then we can go to dinner."

The first E Mail went to the Head of the English Department at SUNY Albany, tendering his resignation effective immediately, and pointing out that she had until Labor Day to find a replacement. The second was addressed to Mike:

Dear Bro:

For sure you finally got your wish. I am now officially on the teaching staff at CCNY. I'll be teaching a couple of summer courses, and I start teaching full time beginning with the fall semester. I'll be able to watch you in person when you play all your home games, and I'll be able to watch my godchildren grow up. I'll be moving in with Andrew as soon as possible. Will let you know daily where we are at. I am happy to sign this note, with love, from Kyle and Andrew.

Kyle pushed the 'send' button and turned to Andrew. "Let's get ready for dinner, and we'll make our plans."

CHAPTER FIVE

They both ordered shrimp dishes. Kyle ordered shrimp scampi and Andrew ordered shrimp with linguini. Both of them delighted in soaking the fresh Italian bread in the sauces. They seemed to have the same taste in everything.

'Here's what I've been thinking," Kyle started. "I live in a rented and furnished studio apartment. I guess I always knew my stay in Albany would be temporary and I never sought to rent anything or buy anything more permanent. If we drive to Albany tomorrow morning in both our cars, I'm positive that I can get all my stuff in the two cars. My books are an exception. I may have to pack some of those up and ship them."

All the time Kyle was talking, Andrew was smiling.

"Did I say something funny?" Kyle asked slightly curious as to why Andrew was looking like a laughing hyena.

"Hell no," Andrew answered. "You said something deeply profound. I live in a rather small two bedroom apartment with one bath. I use the second bedroom as an office. My folks have a large three bedroom apartment with a den and two baths on the Upper East Side. It's where I grew up. Ever since I became a big wage earner, they have been begging me to switch apartments with them. They want me to scale up, and they want desperately to scale down so they can buy a winter place in Florida. This may work out well for us, like you and your new job did. Everything had to wait for the right time to be right for us. We'll just move all your stuff down to me, and live among the clutter until we can make the switch. I'll call my folks tomorrow. Besides asking about the apartment, they keep bugging me about cutting back on my hours and meeting some nice young man to share my life with. I owe it to them to give them the big news."

"Yes, and I'd like to thank them for having had you just for me."

"I know you are a hopeless romantic," Andrew said, "but please don't get mawkish on me."

"Well, I do at least want to tell them what a wonderful son they raised."

"OK, but keep it real," Andrew said, and he squeezed Kyle's hand under the table.

They wanted to get up about four or five in the morning to have a full day in Albany so that night they went to bed without having sex, but they wrapped themselves up in each other's arms, kissing and fondling and crushing their cocks together until they fell asleep.

"If we fall asleep like this every night for the rest of our lives, I'll be a happy man," Kyle said as he dozed off.

"Amen to that," Andrew agreed.

Kyle gave his landlady proper notice and didn't have to pay any additional rent. She applied his security deposit to his final month's rent.

"You were an ideal tenant," she said. "I'll miss you. I keep getting calls from college students asking if I have an empty apartment to rent. I'll probably get stuck with some young hoodlum who'll wreck the place with wild parties and boozing. Well, good luck to you in New York, Dr. Farrell."

In about four hours, they were able to load both cars with all of Kyle's stuff and about half his books. During the time they were packing, Kyle ran down to a mail store and bought sturdy boxes for the excess books. By 2 PM they completed their work and there were five boxes to ship. They had to get a taxi to take them back to the mail store because both cars were loaded.

When that was all done, they realized that they had plenty of time to drive back to the cottage.

"Let's not, just yet," Kyle said. "I want to call a couple of colleagues, and say goodbye. You still have plenty of time to call your folks, but beyond all that mundane stuff, I want to sleep here tonight. When we are old and tottering, I want to be able to say to people, "Yes indeed, Andrew and I made love in every town and in every city we were ever in together.""

"*OY*, you're more than a hopeless romantic. I'll have to coin a new word for whatever it is that you are. For now, I'll just call you a super romantic," Andrew chided.

They sat in the emptied out apartment and Kyle called three colleagues. The conversations were short and it was obvious to Andrew that Kyle had not made any close friends in Albany. Kyle knew what he was thinking and said, "I told you. I always knew I'd be a short timer. I was waiting for you to rescue me."

"Do you mean that you view me as your Prince Charming?"

"Damn right. Now call your folks."

Andrew dialed but he got his parents' answering machine. He told them that he had big news for them, all of it good, and to please call him back on his cell phone. He turned to Kyle and said, "You told Mike all about what's going on with us. How come you haven't mentioned calling your parents?"

Kyle looked distressed. "My parents don't know that I'm gay. Mike has been urging me for years to tell them, but the timing never seemed to be right."

"I don't want to live life as your roommate Kyle. I want to be, I need to be, part of your family and I want you to be part of mine. You should tell them as soon as possible. Why don't you do it right now before you get cold feet?"

Kyle let out a big sigh and called his parents in Rochester. His mother answered. She was so excited to hear his voice. "We just spoke to Mike," she said. "He told us that you were starting a new job and moving to New York. That's wonderful, son. Will you be staying with Mike?" She had no idea how far Manhasset was from CCNY in Upper Manhattan.

"No Ma, I'll be staying with a friend. Mike lives too far away from the college. Ma, is Dad around?"

"Why yes. Do you want to talk to him?"

"I need to talk to both of you at the same time. Could you ask Dad to get on the extension, please?" He waited a long while and finally heard his dad, who sounded out of breath. "Hello sonny, it's great to hear from you."

"It's great to hear your voice, Dad. Are you and ma well?"

"Stop stalling," Andrew whispered to him.

"Hey guys, I need to tell you something. You know the friend in New York that I am going to stay with, well, he's a lot more than my friend. We are in a committed relationship. This has been hard for me to say to you all these years, but now with Andy's support, I want to tell you that I'm gay."

"Well, of course you are, darling," Katie Farrell said.

"I thought that with a PhD you'd be a lot smarter than you are, Dr. Farrell. We've known for years," Warren Farrell said.

Kyle was speechless. "How did you know?"

"Dunno, just knew. You were always so different than your brother. I guess we had what to compare. Are you happy, son?"

"Daddy," (Kyle became a kid again) "I am so happy that there are no words to describe how I feel. I know you never met him, but Andy was Mike's roommate at Syracuse U. Mike wanted to get us together, but it never happened, and then we met accidently, without anybody fixing us up. It was preordained, Dad."

"Preordained or not," Warren said, "you are a couple now. I can't tell you how relieved I am to know that you aren't alone any more. Tell us about Andy."

"First of all he hates to be called Andy by anybody else but me, so try Andrew. He's a rich attorney, and he's a year younger than I, and he expects to be made a partner in his firm within two years. For sure, I know Mike approves of him."

"Can we speak to him? Is he there?"

"Yes, just a sec." He turned toward Andrew and handed him the phone. "They want to talk to you."

"Hi, Mr. and Mrs. Farrell. It's a pleasure."

"Mom and Dad, please," Mrs. Farrell said.

"Welcome to the family," Warren added. "When can we expect to meet you?"

"We have so much to do in the next few weeks. After we plan a schedule, we'll call you and set it up. Maybe you can come to New York and visit Mike and his family at the same time." Andrew's legal brain figured that would sweeten the deal, and get them to visit them instead of vice versa.

'Sounds like a plan," Warren agreed. "Please stay in touch and let us know what's going on, you hear?" Andrew said goodbye to them and handed the phone back to Kyle. He told his folks how much he missed them and how anxious he was for them to meet Andrew, and even before he hung up, the Stanleys called.

After the usual greeting amenities, Andrew said, "I am about to make all your wishes come true."

"Is that so?" his father asked quite doubtfully.

"First of all, I met my soul mate, someone to spend the rest of my life with. I want to be with him so much that I can't possibly work the way I used to, and I know that will make you happy. Second of all, my place is too small for the two of us, so if you still want to swap apartments, we are all for it."

"Wow," Dr. Stanley said. "You sure know how to bowl over your aged parents in just a couple of sentences. What's this Romeo's name and what does he do?" Andrew detected a sound of suspicion from his dad.

"He's not after my money, Dad. Kyle has a doctorate in English Lit. He has been teaching at SUNY Albany, but he just switched to CCNY. He starts teaching there at the end of June."

"When will we meet him?"

"We are in the midst of packing his apartment in Albany and then we'll probably go back to his cabin in the Catskills for a few days before coming home."

"A cabin in the Catskills? Wow, that's fantastic. Do you think we could borrow it sometime?"

"I don't know. Kyle would like to talk to you, so you can ask him yourself." Andrew handed the phone to Kyle. "It's my dad."

"Hello Dr. Stanley. Kyle Farrell, here."

Kyle, if you call me doctor, I'll have to call you doctor. Isn't that pretty awkward to be calling my son-in-law, doctor? If you are uncomfortable calling me Dad and calling my wife Mom, then try Anna and Dave."

"I think I'll go with mom and dad. You can't have too much family."

"I agree. Now about your secluded cabin in the woods, do you....?"

"No need to ask. It's not big enough for all of us, but whenever Andy and I aren't using it, you're free to call it home."

"Excuse me. Did you say Andy?" Warren was incredulous.

"Shit I forgot. I'm the only one allowed to call him that. He wants me to, for some strange reason," Kyle laughed.

"I'll consult my shrink on that one," Dave said. "Kyle, I can't wait to meet you."

"Me too," Anna chirped in. She had been on an extension the whole time.

"Before I hang up," Kyle said, "I need to tell you what a fantastic son you raised. I also want to thank you for having him for me."

"Stop it, Kyle," Anna said. "You'll make me cry."

After they hung up, Andrew said, "You are quite the charmer, Dr. Farrell."

Kyle took Andrew to his favorite restaurant in Albany for dinner; Burger King. Then they went back to the apartment to make love. They were so anxious to touch each other that they decided to play sixty-nine, so they wouldn't have to decide who would 'go first.' They hadn't done that yet, and Kyle pointed out that in their dotage they would remember that the first time they played sixty-nine was in Albany, NY.

"You're the literary member of the family," Andrew pointed out. Why don't you start a journal? It might get published someday like the Mad Housewife or Anais Nin. You can call it Andy and Kyle."

"Terrific idea," Kyle said enthusiastically, "but I think I'll go with Kyle and Andy. I'll want to back track to the day you moored to my dock, and I'll have to include the saga of Carl and Joey. What do you think has happened to them?"

"Nothing good, I'm sure. Now why don't we assume the position?"

The lovers managed to delay their orgasms for almost an hour, and when it was over, Kyle said, "I don't think I could ever get tired of sucking your cock. Your ass is pretty good too."

"Wow! What happened to your florid literary style? *Your ass is pretty good?* My personal Cyrano can do better than that," Andrew said. He grabbed Kyle by the back of his head, pulled him toward him and kissed him passionately until they both fell asleep.

When Andrew woke the next morning, it was still dark, and he was alone in the apartment. He jumped out of bed and turned on the lights. There were two notes from Kyle on Kyle's pillow. The first said that he had gone to McDonald's to get breakfast for them so that they could get going as soon as they ate. The other was a love poem, obviously from Kyle, but attributed to another great poet.

Why Did My Love Choose Me?

By Cyrano de Bergerac

I lay awake at night thinking as hard as I can.
I try to remember what beau geste deed I did
To earn so many Brownie Points
From God.
Whatever valorous act did I do to deserve you?
I'm really not that good, magnificent or saintly
To earn so many Brownie Points
From God.
My beloved, you are far too good for me.
Whatever made you choose and desire me
To earn so many Brownie Points
From God?
I muse and meditate. I try to solve the riddle.
At last it's clear to me and I know why I have
Earned so many Brownie Points
From God.
You took one good look at my enormous cock.
You ogled its size and girth, and desired me.
And now I know why I have
Earned so many Brownie Points
From God.
LOL
CdB

Andrew laughed until his sides hurt. He ran to the bathroom, peed and brushed his teeth. He was dressed before Kyle came home. When he came through the door, Andrew attacked him, smothering him with kisses. "This poem is too funny to ignore. Please put it in your journal."

"Done," Kyle said.

The lovers stayed at the cabin through the Memorial Day weekend. Early Tuesday morning they discarded the perishables, leaving it for the garbage collection. They turned off the water and the electricity, locked up the cabin and got into separate cars. Kyle followed Andrew to Manhattan and to their brand new life. Although the arrangement was temporary, they spent the rest of the week organizing the apartment and making love. They didn't tell anyone that they had returned early.

"I'll go crazy when you go back to work on Monday, "Kyle lamented. "What'll I do?"

"Well, for starters you can begin your journal, and you can hang out with Scott. I love you to pieces, but I don't want to shackle you with vows of monogamy. If you want to play with Scott, it's OK with me, but let me know about it," Andrew said.

"You're very sweet and I appreciate the offer, but I don't want to do any playing with anyone but you. However, how about I call him and we arrange for the three of us to have dinner together this Saturday evening."

"Terrific idea," Andrew said. "We can go to my friend Freddie's place for a lot of reasons. The food there is great; I haven't seen Freddie in a while; and word will get back to Sam that we were at the restaurant. He'll see that we are acting like we are not suspicious of anything, or at least that we are oblivious to his having had any involvement in the matter of Carl and Joey."

"Great idea! You think of everything. I want you to be my lawyer," Kyle joked. "By the way, I've been wondering. How did you ever become good friends with the nephew of Sam Gardini?"

Andrew's first grade class in Upper Manhattan had twenty-five students. Most of them came from broken homes, and these kids had only one parent. Three of the kids had two mommies and one kid had two daddies. Andrew, and only two other classmates, had two parents, a male and a female.

At the first open school night, Mrs. Chessman told Anna Stanley that Andrew was a rarity. Anna thought that she was referring to his academic achievements, and she beamed with pride until Mrs. Chessman added, "Yes, it is such a rarity these days for a child to have two parents, a mother and a father." Well if that made Andrew unique, so be it.

Andrew was a very shy youngster, and at recess on that first day of school, he stood alone in a corner of the school yard and did not join the other students at play. Mrs. Chessman was not one to allow her students to shirk their duties. She walked over to Andrew, took him by the hand and led him to a group of boys playing "Johnny on a Pony."

"Freddie," she called to one of the boys waiting to mount the 'pony,' "why don't you show Andrew how to play the game and see that he joins in?" Freddie walked over to Andrew and Mrs. Chessman walked away.

Freddie really scared Andrew. He was at least three inches taller than he was and much, much broader. His eyes were so blue they were translucent. His face was covered with freckles and his head was matted with the thickest fire red hair that Andrew had ever seen. But when Freddie spoke to him, all the fear left him. Freddie's voice was soft and reassuring and made Andrew feel less threatened.

"I hate this game," Freddie said. "It's dumb and you could break your back. Here, come with me." He led Andrew around a corner. "Mrs. Chessman can't see us from here." Without regard to dirtying his trousers, Freddie sat down on the concrete and leaned against the wall.

"My name's Freddie Grant. What's yours?"

"Andrew Stanley and please don't call me Andy. I hate it."

"That's funny. My name's Alfred and I don't mind being called Freddie at all," Freddie retorted. Andrew ignored him. "Where do you live?" he asked Andrew.

"On E 86th at the corner of Second Ave."

"Is that an apartment building?"

"Uh huh," Andrew nodded.

Then in the smuggest manner, that only a six year old could manage, Freddie announced, "I live in a town house on First and 84th. Would you like to come over sometime after school and play with me?"

"I'll have to ask my mother, but I'm sure she would let me, if your mother lets you," Andrew said. He was really excited at the prospect of having a friend.

"I ain't got a mom," Freddie stated very matter of factly. My folks died in a car accident last year and now I live with my uncle. He's my only relative, and I'm his only relative. My mom was his big sister."

"I'm sorry," Andrew mumbled.

"Don't be. Me and my Uncle get along just great."

Not knowing what to say, Andrew blurted out, "Me and my folks get along pretty good also."

"You said your last name is Stanley. My doctor's name is Stanley. Any relation?" Freddie asked.

"Yup, maybe, he's my dad, I think."

It actually turned out that Freddie went to Andrew's house first. School had been in session for two weeks when they decided to arrange a play date for Friday afternoon. When Anna called the Grant residence, she was surprised that someone answered, "Gardini residence." She asked to speak to Mr. Gardini to see if it was all right to give Freddie cookies with his milk.

"Oh, I'm his nanny and it's perfectly all right. Freddie talks about Andrew all the time."

"I'll get him home before dark. Don't you worry," Anna assured the nanny.

The following Friday Andrew went home with Freddie. When they got there, Freddie's Uncle Sam was at home. He was in his study with the door open so Freddie waited until he was finished with his call before walking in to introduce Andrew.

Uncle Sam was obviously very angry. He yelled into the phone, "Fucking lawyers. They're all the same. It won't do any good to fire this one. The next one will be worse." He slammed down the phone and the boys came in. Even before Freddie could introduce his uncle to his best friend, Andrew said in childish innocence. "Don't be upset Uncle Sam. When I grow up, I'm going to be your lawyer, and I'll be a good one."

Sam could not stop laughing. He scooped up one boy in each arm and twirled around the room with them. He twirled and twirled until he was too dizzy to stand. He put the boys down, and collapsed on a chair.

After that, Sam took Andrew everywhere he took Freddie. They went to the zoo, ball games, museums and even musical theater. Freddie particularly enjoyed the fine restaurants Uncle Sam took them to, because he secretly yearned to be a chef. The boys were so close to Sam that when they were teenagers, they came out to him even before Andrew told his parents. Sam Gardini and Freddie Grant were Andrew's second family.

"And you have been friends ever since you first met?" Kyle asked.

"Yup. Remember I told you that I whacked off with a friend in high school. It was Freddie. We have never touched each other. We grew up like brothers and unlike Carl and Joey, we can't imagine doing each other."

"Yuck, the thought of doing Mike is a yuck also," Kyle agreed.

Kyle called Scott and they made arrangements to meet at "Freddie's Surf and Turf" on Columbus Avenue on Saturday evening at 7:30 PM. When the date was set, Andrew called Freddie. The phone was answered by a reservationist, and she took the reservation. She did not hesitate to put Andrew through to Freddie when he asked to speak to the big kahuna. She was aware of their relationship, but she erroneously thought that it was sexual.

"About fucking time you called," Freddie chided Andrew. "Why didn't you tell me you were going on vacation? I maybe would have gone with you, and we could have gone cruising together."

"Trust me, there was no place to cruise, and the experience was a bummer. I told Uncle Sam about it, and I'll tell you when I see you Saturday evening. We're coming for dinner."

"Who is 'we?'" Freddie inquired.

"Someone special I want you to meet, and his boss. You better be kind to us on the check. They're school teachers and don't make a helluva lot of money."

"Special for you, babe, I'll give you a 10% discount on the 100% inflated price."

"Very funny! Seriously, I can't wait to see you and give you all the news. I love you."

CHAPTER SIX

When Andrew and Kyle arrived at Freddie's restaurant, they checked in with Kim at the front reception desk. Scott was already there. He was seated at the bar sipping a scotch and soda. They sauntered over to the bar to join him. Before Kyle could even introduce Andrew, Scott said, "Christ Kyle, why didn't you tell me how good looking your main squeeze is? Hell, I don't stand a chance."

"My *only* squeeze," Kyle corrected him.

"Whatever. It's nice to meet you, Andrew." Scott stuck out his hand to shake Andrew's, and without missing a beat, he asked, "How do you get Kyle's monster cock inside you every day? I'm still hurting from eight years ago."

It was a tense moment until Andrew laughed and said. "It gets easier every day." They ordered drinks, and moved to a small table in the bar area. Scott and Kyle talked mostly about the summer courses Kyle was about to teach. Andrew sat by and listened.

It did not surprise him; in fact, he expected it to happen. He looked up and there was Uncle Sam coming into the bar. Andrew was prepared for that, but he began to get stomach cramps when he saw that Sam was accompanied by two bulky dudes. There was no question in his mind that he had seen them before.

Andrew didn't wait for Sam to see him. He jumped up and ran over to his uncle. He threw his arms around Sam and the two men kissed each other on both cheeks. The two men accompanying Sam stood politely back. Sam made no attempt to introduce them.

"Come, Uncle, I want you to meet Kyle."

"I can't wait."

Kyle and Scott had witnessed this scene of greeting and had stopped talking. Andrew was holding Sam's hand as he walked him back to their table.

"It gives me great pleasure, Uncle, to introduce you to Dr. Kyle Farrell, and to Dr. Scott Johnson. Scott's the head of the English Department at CCNY."

"The pleasure is all mine. I don't want to intrude on your dinner gentlemen, so I'll just say to Kyle that we will get together soon and learn all about each other. It's wonderful to have another nephew and to see Andrew so happy and settled at last." Sam turned to Andrew. "Before you sit down to dinner can I speak to you alone for just a minute, Andrew?" Kyle's stomach flipped and Andrew's legs buckled.

"Sure, Uncle Sam. Is anything wrong? Can I help you with something?"

Sam led Andrew to a table in the corner of the bar and indicated that he should sit. "It's about Freddie," he said. "I'd appreciate if you would talk to him."

"Of course, Uncle. What about?"

"Andrew, my boy, nobody knows better than you and my accountant how wealthy I am. This restaurant is a great little place and Freddie has made it very successful, but he's my only heir. I want him to prepare himself to take over all my various business enterprises. Hell, he doesn't have to give up the restaurant. He can add it to the other businesses that he'll be running, but he keeps turning me down."

"Wow, Uncle Sam, I know how important this is to you and I promise I'll have a long talk with him. I can't say if I'll be successful, but I swear I'll try."

"Here's something to sweeten the deal," Sam added. Tell him that if he agrees, I'm going to leave a percentage to you too. Knowing that you'll be his partner, someone he can lean on and depend on, he might just change his mind."

"Uncle Sam I don't know what to say. That's too generous."

"Nonsense! You're like a son to me. Andrew there's one other thing, and you are the perfect person to speak to Freddie about this. Lately he has been dating boys who look like jail bait to me. Freddie assures me they are legal, but I feel like I want to check their driver's licenses. He's seeing a young kid now. He's a real punk, and I'm sure he sees Freddie as a sugar daddy. Try to talk some sense into him. Maybe there's someone you could introduce Freddie to that has some substance. That's why I am so happy about you and Kyle. You're both mature and ready for a relationship, and you're an excellent role model for Freddie."

"Uncle Sam, you are putting a big burden on my shoulders, but I assure you, I will do my best. Certainly I'd like to see Freddie in a relationship and as happy as I am."

"I see that Kim is seating Kyle and Scott so I'll let you go. Before I do, look at those two hefty guys over there? If you ever see either of them or both of them hanging around you in a crowd, don't be frightened. After what happened to you in the Catskills, I've instructed them to watch over you, Kyle and Freddie, sort of like bodyguards."

"Uncle Sam, that really isn't necessary."

"I say it is, so let's not argue. Now go and enjoy dinner. I'm having dinner with your bodyguards. They're cousins by the way, Manuel and Jorge Rodriguez. If you ever need them, and you are in a crowd but you can't see them, you can call out their names and they'll come running." Sam stood up and Andrew knew that it was time to split. Again they kissed on the cheeks, and Andrew ran to his table. Kim was just leaving when he got there, and their waiter was approaching.

"Why is the table set for four?" Andrew asked.

"Apparently Freddie is joining us for dinner and leaving things to his sous chef," Kyle said.

"Unbelievable," Andrew said. "I never thought that he would delegate anything."

"What was that all about with Sam?" Kyle wanted to know.

"Later," Andrew whispered. "Don't worry it wasn't about the other thing."

The waiter suggested another round of drinks since it would be a few more minutes before Freddie could join them. He said that they might as well order the drinks because Freddie's Uncle Sam was paying for them. All three looked over at Sam's table and mouthed, "Thank you."

Finally Freddie came running over. He was dressed casually; all evidence of his chef's attire was discarded. He and Andrew kissed each other on the lips and then Andrew made introductions. It was obvious to Kyle and Andrew that there was more than a spark of interest shown when Freddie and Scott shook hands. By the time the entrée was served, Scott and Freddie might as well have been seated at separate tables.

Is it possible that these two relationship challenged friends might actually be interested in each other? Andrew wondered. He could only hope.

From across the room, the sharp eyes of Sam Gardini noticed also, and he was inwardly pleased. It suddenly occurred to him that if Freddie was in a stable and loving relationship, he might be more willing to take on his business responsibilities as well. At one point he caught Andrew's eye and they both smiled and nodded at each other.

During dessert, Andrew asked Freddie to please come up to his office late in the morning on Monday. "Uncle Sam has some serious stuff he wants me to talk to you about. We can have lunch and discuss it."

"I know what it's about and it's a waste of time."

"Let's at least talk about it; it can't hurt," Andrew pleaded. Freddie nodded in resignation.

By the time the meal was over, Freddie asked Scott to please wait for him until he closed the restaurant at 11 PM. Scott agreed, so Kyle and Andrew got up to leave. At the same time, Sam's chauffer was leading Sam to his car, but the Rodriguez cousins remained at the table. Andrew had no doubt that one of them would 'escort' Kyle and him home. He hoped that Kyle would not notice. The other one would be keeping an eye on Freddie. That was pretty rotten inconsiderate stuff for a guy looking to get laid that night. Andrew could only imagine at how far the bodyguards would go in 'keeping an eye on them.'

Freddie got to Andrew's office at 11:45 Monday morning. When they were alone in Andrew's private office, he grabbed Andrew, wrapped him in a bear hug, and kissed him on the lips. Freddie was bigger than Andrew, but not nearly as big as Kyle. Nevertheless, his bear hug did nothing for Andrew's ribs.

"Careful," he said. "Are you trying to create another Eve?"

Freddie pulled back. "I can't thank you enough for introducing me to Scott," he said.

"I'm surprised you feel that way. What about all your little boy toys?"

"That's the point. Toys are for playing and tossing away. I feel Scott is a keeper. By the way isn't that what you want to talk to me about, settling down?"

"Yes, that's one of the things."

"OK, mark that one done. Scott and I are more or less 'going steady.' Now let's go to lunch and you can barrage me with the other stuff."

After laying everything on the table, the lunch table so to speak, Freddie whispered to Andrew, "Look Bro, you know that I'm not afraid of running all of Uncle Sam's businesses that file income tax returns. We both know it's the other stuff that I really don't want to get involved with."

"I know exactly how you feel. Sam offered me a percentage also. He feels that if we are active partners, you might be more inclined to give it more thought. Besides, once we have control we can divest ourselves of the other stuff, as you refer to it."

Freddie grabbed Andrew's hand and squeezed it. That reaction was the most intimate thing that they had ever done together. Even after realizing that they were both gay when they were teenie boppers, they had not been intimate. Not even when they whacked off together, had they so much as touched the other.

"Uncle Sam offered you part of the business too?" Freddie asked with a tear in his eye. "That does give me pause to think about it a little more. I'd feel differently with you at my side to help me and to guide me. And like you said, we could get rid of the other stuff. Besides, if I do settle down with Scott, I would like more normal hours. I wouldn't want to do the cooking at the restaurant anymore."

When they got up to leave, they embraced and kissed each other on the lips as they always did, but this time Andrew was aware that Freddie's lips were slightly open and so were his. He felt funny about that, but soon dismissed it from his mind. Freddie went back to his restaurant and Andrew returned to his office. He immediately dialed Sam and made an appointment with him at Sam's office for the first thing the following morning.

That evening at dinner, Andrew told Kyle that he was seeing Sam the next morning, mainly about Freddie. "But also, I'm tired of being afraid of how he would react if he knew we knew those goons worked for him. Would he be afraid we would turn him in for murdering them, and then in turn would he have us rubbed out? I'm going to tell him that we know, how we found out, and that we fully approve seeing as how those animals raped us. I'll also point out that we have a lawyer-client relationship and I can't be forced to reveal anything I know about him. I know he'll be OK with it."

"I also feel that we can't live in fear that he'll find out. Do what you think is best, darling." Kyle said, giving Andrew permission to speak to Sam.

Andrew did not sleep all night. He kept rehearsing over and over again what he would say to Sam, and how he would say it. Nothing definitive enough satisfied him and he just let it go. He decided to just play it by ear.

Andrew was literally shaking when he walked into Sam's office in the morning. Sam got out from behind his desk and embraced Andrew. He kissed him on both cheeks as he usually did, and he beckoned him to be seated. Sam didn't say anything so Andrew began.

"I had lunch with Freddie yesterday, and it's all good. First of all, he and Scott are dating. Scott's a little older than Freddie, but that's fine. A mature man, with a career, will be good for Freddie, I think. He realizes that the boy toys were for fun and sex, but he really wants to settle down now. Probably turning thirty was his eye opener."

Sam laughed. "Yeah," he agreed it's a shocker for all of us."

"So it's looking good for a solid relationship to develop. I guess it took Scott into his forties to realize the same awful truth. You can't burn the candle at both ends forever and expect to have any candle left," Andrew added.

"Amen to that," Sam agreed.

Andrew continued. "He seemed dead set against inheriting your business empire until I told him that you had offered me a percentage. Then he backed down a lot. He felt that with me there to help him and also to guide him, it might work. We always made a good pair. Anyway, he agreed that the picture was changed a lot and that he would give it serious thought. I guess you can expect to hear from him soon."

"Oh, Andrew," I knew I could depend on you. You're my rock."

"Sam, there is one other thing I must talk to you about. Can you give me another few minutes?"

"Why of course. It sounds serious."

"It's either serious or not worth mentioning. It's all up to you Sam."

"Shoot away, son. I'm listening."

"Sam, I've kept a secret from you. I didn't want to, but you'll understand why, when I tell it to you."

Andrew did not want to drag it out. He wanted to blurt it out and get it over with. He walked over to Sam's desk and spotted the note pad with Sam's name engraved on the top. He removed one sheet of paper, and showed it to Sam.

"Uncle Sam," Andrew began. "I know that you have other business interests that I'm not privy to. I don't know the details, and I don't want to know until you feel secure enough with me to trust me. Don't forget, we have lawyer-client immunity. That having been said, I believe the two guys who rescued Kyle and me at the cabin are the Rodriguez cousins. When I met them at Freddie's restaurant, I was pretty certain that they were the ones." Sam remained silent.

"Carl and Joey were naked when your men barged in, and then they all disappeared rather quickly. They neglected to take the twins' clothes so Kyle and I decided to destroy it and not leave any evidence. As a lawyer, I should have felt differently. I should have insisted that we report the incident to the police and turn over the evidence. But a sixth sense, and terrible shame at having been raped, turned my thinking around. To make a long story short, Uncle Sam, in one of the trouser pockets, I found this note paper with your name on it, and directions to an address in Englewood, NJ. I knew immediately that Joey and Carl had betrayed your trust in some way or other, and that the Rodriguez cousins had caught up to them. I wanted to kiss your feet for rescuing us, but at the same time I was afraid of how you would feel knowing that I know the whole scenario. Now that I have unburdened myself, there are no more secrets between us, Uncle Sam. I would go to prison myself before I would betray you. I love you too much."

The room was silent for a long while. Andrew had buried his head in his hands and was weeping silently. Sam walked over to Andrew's chair and stood him up. He put his arms around his adopted nephew, rested Andrew's head on his shoulder, and whispered softly in Andrew's ear, "When I heard what those two bastards did to you and Kyle, I wanted to strangle them with my own two hands. I love you too, my son, and I trust you completely. I am so happy you told me your little secret. I did wonder if the twins had revealed anything to you. Now I can stop wondering, and you and Kyle can stop worrying. You and Freddie are my heirs, and I see only a bright future for all of us.

Sam leaned down and kissed Andrew on the lips. It was more than a fatherly peck. There was a lot of passion in it, and Andrew responded by parting his lips and kissing Sam back.

Sam's father Louie (Luigi) was a first generation American. He had to work hard in the days following World War II. As a young teenager, he got a job running numbers for a petty thief. The guy was stupid and it didn't take Louie very long to figure out how to cut in on his territory. After that, it was only a matter of time before Jake Goldman was out of business. Little by little, Louie expanded his enterprises. At first it was only gambling, then a little prostitution and finally drugs.

When he was twenty-five, he agreed to an arranged marriage only because he wanted to have a son to inherit all that he had strived for and had achieved. He was disappointed when his first born was a girl. In time, however, he learned to love Maria. She was pretty and had a very sweet disposition. Louie's prayers were answered four years later with the birth of his son Samuel. Sam was a strong baby and grew into a healthy adult. From the time Sam was in kindergarten, Louie took him on his 'rounds' with him. By ten, Sam knew the nature of all of his father's enterprises. He knew which businesses he could talk about, and which were taboo to speak of. He knew every person who worked for his father and the pecking order of each. Some were promising business men and others were losers.

One of the losers was Gerald Grant. He had come to America from Scotland and was here only a couple of years when he went to work for Louie. Louie liked him and gave him odd jobs, but he wasn't too bright and his chores were limited. Nevertheless, at seventeen, he was built like a brick shithouse and he had his eye on Maria, who was nearing seventeen. Maria was blinded by Gerald's good looks and got herself knocked up on her seventeenth birthday. They married in haste. When Freddie was born, Sam was only fourteen. His relationship with Freddie was more that of an older brother than an uncle.

When Sam was fifteen, Louie felt secure enough in Sam's abilities that he finally decided to take a vacation, leaving Sam to run things. He and Sam's mother got in the family car and started off to Atlantic City. Somewhere along the way, the couple disappeared, never to be seen again. Even the car was never found. Sam knew who his father's enemies were. Some of them worked for his father, and he had tried to warn him, but Louie was too trusting. At this point in his life, Sam trusted nobody and vowed to take revenge all by himself.

Of course, business declined considerably with the boss gone. But there were a slew of unsolved murders happening in and around New York City, and after each one there was a sudden surge in Sam's profits. His enemies foolishly assumed that a fifteen year old boy would fall by the wayside, but during the next year, Sam silently stalked everyone he thought might be responsible for his parent's death. He studied their habits and knew exactly when they would be the most vulnerable. He took his revenge personally, silently and quickly. When those in the know realized how firmly Sam had taken over and rescued the business, and how swiftly he had eradicated any signs of poaching, they all stepped back. They feared Sam to the point that nobody dared cross him.

When little Freddie, the apple of Sam's eye, was nearing his fifth birthday, Sam's sister, Maria, came to him. She begged him to give Gerald better work to do so he could earn more money. "After all," she pointed out. It was for Freddie's benefit. The only money his sister had was Gerald's earnings. Louie had been wise enough to leave Maria's inheritance in a trust fund that she couldn't touch until her 28th birthday. He confided in Sam that he thought Gerald was too stupid to trust him with all that money.

Sam had a slew of cash businesses; video arcades, Laundromats, sports bars, etc. He reluctantly gave Gerald the job of collecting the cash at these places, and he generously raised his salary far beyond what the service was worth. Things went well for several weeks until Sam's in-house accountant pointed out that receipts at each establishment were steadily declining. Sam had no choice but to put a tail on Gerald and he even bugged his sister's apartment.

Each evening after work, Gerald delivered a sack of money from each business to Sam's office. He went directly home from there. When he parked his car, he removed two or three paper bags from the trunk. He rushed into his apartment where he and Maria counted the money. Maria marked something (presumably the amount) in a small ledger and put all the money in one bag before they went to bed.

The following morning, Maria put Freddie in a stroller and covered his legs with a blanket even in warm weather. She put the bag under the blanket and headed for a bank two blocks away. The bank had a machine, which counted the money for a fee and then printed out a receipt for the net amount. Marie then prepared a deposit slip for the amount on the receipt. One morning as she was preparing the receipt a woman stood quite close by to her.

"What a cute baby. I've never seen hair so red," the woman said. Maria was distracted for the moment and the woman clearly read the name on the deposit slip, John and Mary Smith.

The following week, Sam gave Gerald and Maria a terrific gift. He presented them with a weekend at a honeymoon resort in the Poconos. They were thrilled and got even more excited when Sam told them that he had hired a nanny, and he would baby sit Freddie over the weekend.

The following Friday afternoon, Sam and the nanny picked up Freddie. They all waved goodbye to his parents as they drove off to Pennsylvania. At the first gas station, Gerald and Marie used the wash rooms and when they got back in the car, they failed to see the Rodriguez twins crouched in the back of the car. Unexpectedly the car left the highway and turned off onto a dirt road. Somehow, the car did not negotiate the dirt road well and crashed into an old tree bursting instantly into flames. Only two bodies were found, Freddie's parents.

After Gerald and Maria left, Sam sent Freddie and the nanny home in his car. He let himself into his sister's apartment with a passkey and found a book of checks with the name of John and Mary Smith on it. He walked calmly into the bank, and asked a teller for the balance in this account.

"$20,250.55," she said. "Mr. Smith, you really shouldn't keep such a large balance in a non-interest bearing account."

"I know," Sam said. "I intend to withdraw the money to pay for a good investment that I am purchasing." Sam prepared a check for $20,250.55 payable to Samuel Gardini. The teller asked for ID and he produced a phony driver's license with the name John Smith on it.

He left the bank, and took a cab to his bank. All the customer service reps knew him and they jumped when they saw him. Even though he was only nineteen years old, they practically attacked each other to serve him. Sam opened a money market college fund account in the name of Alfred Grant. He even knew Freddie's social security number.

As soon as word reached him of his sister's death, Sam called a judge who was on his payroll, and immediately obtained guardianship of his nephew, Freddie. The judge entirely overlooked the fact that Sam himself was a minor. He was just a few months shy of his 20th birthday.

Freddie was the only person in Sam's life. He had no girlfriends, and in fact discouraged any relationships. When he felt the need, he went through the names of the prostitutes he had on his payroll. They were billed out as escorts of course. When he found a name that intrigued him, like Daisy La Fleur for instance, he would have her sent around for the night. He enjoyed the sex with these girls, but was never really satisfied.

One day looking down the list, he spotted the name Jean Gay. Amused by the name, he sent for her, only to find out that Jean was a nineteen year old boy. They were the same age. Sam forgot that he employed male prostitutes as well as females, for those so inclined.

When Jean spotted Sam, he was so eager to get going, he was practically salivating. It was rare for a client to be so young and handsome. Sam didn't have the heart to send him away. Also, he was curious as to what would happen.

"Aren't you going to undress?" Jean asked. He was already almost naked.

"Sure, sure," Sam said. He stripped quickly and got into bed. Jean was already there.

"What do you like to do?" Jean asked.

"I'll leave it to you to make me happy. I've never been with a man before."

"I promise that you won't be disappointed." Jean cuddled up to Sam and started to kiss him. Sam was shocked and turned away. "My kisses are sweeter than any woman's. Don't resist me. Just follow my lead and you will be one happy dude before we're done." So Sam kissed Jean back. The more passionate Jean became, the more Sam did also. Before he knew what was happening Sam was kissing Jean as if they were lovers, and he wanted so much more. Jean began to work his way down Sam's body. He kissed his ears, his nipples, his navel and he finally started to lick at his balls and tease his cock with an occasional swipe of his tongue up Sam's eight inch uncut cock.

Sam hated to admit it, but he was more aroused than he had been with any of the women he had ever been with. Jean continued by taking as much of Sam into his mouth as possible. Sam had never known such rapture. The wet warm feeling of Jean's tongue suckling his cock and occasionally his balls was almost more than he could bear. Then abruptly Jean stopped sucking and jumped out of bed. Sam's cock waved at the ceiling, resentful of the interruption. Jean took something out of a small bag he had brought with him. It was a condom and a tube of lube. He rolled the condom down Sam's cock. Sam moaned at the erotic feelings he was having as the condom rolled down his rod. Then Jean took some lube and generously swabbed Sam's cock with it and then he greased his own ass. Sam's cock tweaked in anticipation.

Jean straddled Sam and positioned his ass hole above Sam's dick. Slowly he lowered himself allowing the big cock to enter him. There was little resistance. When he was all the way in, Jean rested. Shortly thereafter, he started to pump up and down. It didn't take Sam long to capture the rhythm and work with Jean. He kept sighing with great moans of extreme pleasure. Jean could sense that Sam was near and he pumped harder and harder. Then with a shriek, Sam came. Jean kept pumping, but eventually Sam had to stop him. Only when Sam got soft did Jean rise off of him. They both got out of bed and showered together. They discreetly tried not to touch one another, but Sam really wanted to fondle Jean.

They dried off and Jean asked Sam if he could stay the night or if Sam wanted him to go. Sam answered by patting his bed, indicating that Jean should lie down with him. As soon as they were both in bed together, primal instinct took over. They turned toward each other, wrapped their arms around each other and began to kiss. After a while, Sam asked Jean what cock tasted like and what it felt like to have a cock up your ass.

"It's heavenly," Jean answered. "Would you like to find out for yourself?"

Without hesitating, Sam said, "Yes," and he immediately realized that he was a queer. There was no doubt about it. He wanted to eat cock and take dick up his ass. Strangely, the realization did not bother him in the least. He leaned right over and began to lick on Jean's six inch circumcised cock. He licked up and down to discover that it was soft on the outside and rock hard inside. This phenomenon gave him extreme pleasure. Finally, he took it into his mouth. This tasted better than pussy and he was really enjoying the whole experience. When Jean felt himself cumming, he stopped Sam and made him roll onto his stomach. He lay on top of Sam with his cock jabbing Sam's ass cheeks. Then Sam felt a sensation that made his head spin. Jean was licking Sam's crack up and down and occasionally entering it with his tongue.

"Aah, aah," Sam sighed. "It's too good. Give me the real thing."

Jean put on a condom, greased Sam's ass and his own cock and began his entry doggie style. Sam screamed once as Jean invaded his sphincter, but when he was inside, the pain abated. Jean's cock was rubbing against Sam's prostate and he was screaming in pleasure. More shockingly, he was cumming again. The two young men got off together. Jean collapsed on top of Sam and neither could move for a long while.

They fell asleep wrapped up together. About three in the morning, Sam was awakened by the sensation of his dick being bathed in warm, moist water. Jean was sucking his cock. It didn't take him long to cum once again. Jean swallowed all Sam's spunk, and when Sam wondered out loud how it tasted, Jean told him he was more than welcome to find out. With the new knowledge that he was indeed homosexual, Sam was eager to experience cum draining down his throat, and he immediately went down on Jean.

After that first glorious evening, he had Jean come around often, and eventually the two men fell in love. In his position, Sam could never allow himself to be outed so he hired Jean to be his driver and his valet. Jean appeared to be a humble employee, but Sam saw to it that Jean became wealthy in his own right. Jean was also another spying eye within Sam's stable of employees. Neither Andrew nor Freddie ever suspected the truth, that's how discreet Sam and Jean were. For his part, Sam secretly reveled in the pride and openness of his two nephews.

CHAPTER SEVEN

In the weeks to come, Kyle's parents came from Rochester for a visit. They stayed in Mike's huge house, of course, and Mike made a big family dinner. How different things were now. Mike embraced Andrew and kissed him on the lips. He lamented that they had not been better friends in college, but vowed to make up for it now. He and Kyle lavished Mike's children with gifts, and the children won Andrew's heart.

One week later, Andrew's sister and her husband made a big family dinner, and Kyle got to meet his in-laws. Sharon had two children also and they bombarded these two with gifts as well. Kyle fell in love with his new niece and nephew.

But the truth is that for better or worse, they were really members of the Gardini family. After Freddie announced that Scott and he were committing to each other, Sam arranged for a lavish family dinner at The Four Seasons.

"Would you mind if I ask Jean to join us tonight?" Sam asked Freddie and Scott, as if they had the decision making vote.

"Of course, not, Unc. Jean is like one of the family as far as I'm concerned," Freddie said.

"Yes, he's very fond of you and Andrew. So it will be the six of us."

Everyone had too much to drink except Jean. Scott and Freddie had agreed to spend the night in Freddie's old quarters in Sam's house, and Jean would be driving them all home as the designated driver. Sam had arranged for a cab to drive Andrew and Kyle home. They were still living downtown in Andrew's old place, but they were moving the following Thursday.

In the weeks to come it took a great deal of coaxing on Sam's part, but he got Scott and Freddie to agree to give up both their tiny apartments, and move into his spacious town house. Sam's bedroom was downstairs, and Jean occupied a small bedroom next to Sam's. The two bedrooms had a connecting door, but that did not arouse suspicion. Everyone expected Jean to be at Sam's beck and call 24 hours a day.

The entire upper floor, two bedrooms and two baths, would belong to Scott and Freddie. This assured them perfect privacy. Sam reminded them that the house would be Freddie's someday anyway. He sweetened the deal by telling them that they would have no rent to pay, and that they need only share the utilities with him. The final argument was that CCNY was a short drive away, and when he was available, Jean could drive Scott to work. How could the new lovers refuse the offer?

Andrew's apartment switch with his parents was more difficult. It took careful planning and tricky logistics. Since Sam owned the moving company, they got priority treatment and attention. The moving trucks were loaded at the same time, and the one that was loaded first waited for the second to be finished before unloading. Naturally, there was no extra charge for the dockage. Everyone was settling into a routine and Andrew and Kyle almost forgot about their ordeal with Carl and Joey, and the manner in which the twins met their demise.

One Monday morning Andrew got a call from Sam. "Good morning, Unc. What's up?"

"I have wonderful, wonderful news!!!" Sam fairly shouted. Last night I had a long talk with Freddie. I asked Scott to be present and I finally convinced him to take over my businesses. I told him that I wanted to start slowing down almost immediately. Of course, he said that he would only do it with you as his partner."

"That's wonderful, Uncle Sam. I am so happy for you, but you're only 44. I can't even imagine you slowing down. Why you and Scott are the same age."

Andrew could only wonder at Scott's reaction. His modest salary as a professor, even as head of the department, could not come close to comparing to the wealth he had married into. Andrew was relatively certain that he knew nothing of Sam's side ventures.

"How did Scott react to it all?" Andrew asked out of curiosity.

"I think he was too dumbfounded to react to anything, but he was very pleased for Freddie. Anyway, I'd like to come up to your office as soon as possible and lay out the details with you, so that you can begin to prepare the necessary paper work."

"That's wonderful, Uncle Sam." Andrew said. "Is 11 AM today convenient for you? We can work through lunch if we have to."

"Perfect. I'll see you then."

Sam's business ventures were vast and widespread. They extended beyond the United States into Canada, Mexico and Europe. It took Andrew almost two months to complete the paper work. If he had not had the help of a bright young law clerk, it would have taken twice as long. Andrew and Freddie were to receive 48% each of Sam's business assets. Freddie had told Sam that he would refuse to take anything unless he and Andrew received equal shares. Sam would retain 4% and upon his death, the remaining shares would go equally to Freddie and Andrew. Upon the death of either of Sam's nephews, their shares would go to the other.

Andrew prepared documents for only the legitimate businesses. There was an aura of vagueness surrounding what would happen to Sam's other ventures. Andrew didn't dare ask, and he hoped Sam would continue to control and run these enterprises, but in his heart he knew that Sam planned for his nephews to take over these businesses sub rosa someday.

When all the documents were ready, and Andrew had read and reread them a thousand times, he called Sam. "We three have to sign everything in triplicate. It will take hours to get through it all. I thought you might want to do all this in your study at home. It will be more comfortable for all of us, and we can more readily break for lunch. If you agree, I'll need some help to bring everything over."

"Not a problem, I'll send Manuel and Jorge over to your office with a car. They'll help you, and your precious cargo, get here."

On the evening before the signing, as they were getting ready for bed, Scott could see how nervous and jumpy Freddie was. "I know just what you need to calm down," Scott said.

"Are you going to do all the work tonight?" Freddie asked with a leer.

"Sure, if that's what you want, but what I actually had in mind, was a glass of white wine. I know how wine always relaxes you and makes you sleepy."

"That's a great idea," Freddie said. "Since you are doing all the work, I don't mind getting tired and sleepy."

They were already naked, so Scott grabbed a robe and headed down stairs to the kitchen. They always kept at least one bottle of white wine in the fridge for chilling. Halfway down the stairs, he could see that there was a light on in the kitchen. Sam had retired early so Scott was a little surprised. He proceeded down the stairs more slowly and more cautiously. Near the bottom of the staircase, he got a partial view of the kitchen. Jean was standing at the sink totally naked.

Nice butt, Scott thought. Jean had just poured two glasses of beer. He took one in each hand, and turned to leave the kitchen. Scott could now see all of Jean in full frontal nudity. Scott knew that he, Sam and Jean were all the same age, and he was glad to see that Jean's body remained as firm and youthful as his own. He wondered if Sam could say the same. Sam had a fully equipped exercise room in the basement and all four occupants of the house used the facility whenever they could.

Jean flipped the kitchen light switch with his elbow. The kitchen was now dark. This allowed Scott to see a light coming from Sam's room. He went to the bottom of the stairs where he could now see that Sam's bedroom door was open. He could see Sam sitting naked on a chair, which was near his bed. Jean came into the room. He placed the two beer glasses on Sam's night table, and then he leaned over and kissed Sam. He got on his knees and began to suck Sam's cock. Scott could now see that Sam's dick was huge, almost as big as Kyle's. Scott was frozen to the bottom stair. He didn't want to move and make his presence known. He was just about to retreat up the stairs, when Jean stood up and closed the door. A moment later, the light coming through the bottom of the door became black. It didn't take a rocket science, or a PhD for that matter, to know what was happening behind the closed door.

As quietly as possible, he poured a glass of wine for Freddie and went back to their bedroom. The first thing he did when he entered the room was close the door. His mind was racing overtime. Should he tell Freddie or keep it his secret? He decided to say nothing, at least for the moment. Instead he thought he would begin to pay very close attention in the future, to how Jean and Sam interacted in an everyday setting.

Freddie was half through his glass of wine and considerably more relaxed. "Aren't you going down on me as promised, professor?" he asked.

Scott climbed into bed. "Not tonight love," he informed Freddie. "I've kinda lost it for the moment."

It's really too bad that Scott did not inform Freddie of what he saw. Had he done so, Freddie would have been better prepared for what happened after he and Andrew signed all the documents the next day.

Manuel and Jorge arrived at Andrew's office promptly at 8:30 AM the next morning. When they got off the elevator, three big boxes were sitting on the floor waiting for them. They each carried one and Andrew carried the other. The car was in front of the building in a no parking zone. Manuel was able to fit two boxes in the trunk of the car. He placed the third on the back seat so that it shared the short ride with Andrew.

When they arrived at the Town House, Jorge told Andrew to go right in and that he and Manuel would take the boxes to Sam's study. Andrew started up the steps to the front door just as Scott was leaving. The two friends kissed each other on the lips, and for a brief moment Scott thought of detaining Andrew and telling him what he had seen the evening before. At the last second, he thought better of it and just told Andrew to go straight to the kitchen. Jean had prepared breakfast for all of them. He rushed off to the corner to hail a cab to take him to the college.

After breakfast, Sam, Freddie and Andrew went into Sam's study, and Andrew invited Jean to join them because they needed a witness to the signatures. Jean was very surprised and exceptionally pleased that Andrew didn't mind his being privy to family secret matters. He entered last and discreetly closed the door. Then he seated himself unobtrusively in a corner.

Andrew had stacked the documents in the three boxes in the order they would be signed. He removed the first packet and spent a few minutes explaining the contents. Sam asked a few questions and was satisfied with the answers. Each packet represented one of the businesses. It contained three identical copies of the contract sealed in plastic folders. The interested parties signed in triplicate and Jean witnessed all three triplicates. Andrew placed each copy of the first packet face down on the floor in three separate stacks, and retrieved the next packet of papers. The process was repeated over and over until the contents of the first box was completely executed and witnessed.

When they were nearly through the second carton, they took a break and Jean made ham and cheese sandwiches for lunch, which he served with lemonade. "This isn't much of a lunch," Sam complained. "This occasion calls for a real celebration. Freddie, call your restaurant and book six for seven. Then call Kyle and Scott and tell them to meet us there for a celebration dinner." Both Andrew and Freddie assumed that the sixth person would be Jean and they were happy about that. He had been around almost since Freddie moved in with his uncle and he was every bit a part of the family.

It was almost 5 PM when everything was done. Jean, Andrew and Freddie took the first pile of folders and placed them in one of the boxes. They did the same for the second and third pile. "The first box is for you, Uncle Sam, and the second is for you, Freddie. I guess you can get them into a vault or file them in some other safe place. The first chance I get, I'll take the third box home, and figure out where to stow it. I also have unsigned copies in my office files."

Sam was sitting quietly behind his desk, and although he was smiling broadly, he had tears in his eyes. "My boys, you have made me so happy. Words cannot express how I feel today. He stood up and held out his arms. Freddie let Sam wrap his right arm around his shoulder, and Andrew let him wrap his left arm around his shoulder. Sam pulled them close, hugging them tightly and then he kissed each one in turn. Gone were the chaste kisses on the cheek. First, he pressed hard against Freddie's lips, parting them with his tongue. Freddie began to respond to this passionate kiss and then realized that this kind of kiss was usually a prelude to sex. It would be an understatement to say that he was very confused.

Sam let go of Freddie and repeated the process with Andrew. Sam had kissed Andrew with his tongue on the day Andrew told him that he knew about Joey and Carl, so he wasn't as surprised as Freddie. He too instinctively responded to Sam's passionate kisses. Sam was holding both of his heirs so tightly that he could feel both of their erections on his thighs. He took his sweet time and finally released them. It was clear that he too had an erection.

"Now," he said to Andrew and Freddie, "kiss your brother." The two new millionaires faced each other and smiled broadly. Then they grabbed each other and kissed wildly and passionately. Their tongues dueled and their erections rubbed hard against each other. For the first time in their lives, they wanted each other. They were consumed with lust. Hell, they both wanted Uncle Sam also. Only the sound of Sam's voice broke them up.

"Now, grab some chairs and sit down. I have something to tell you." He looked at Andrew. "Andrew, we promised each other that we would never have a secret between us again, and now it's my turn to confess my final secret."

Freddie was disturbed. When did his brother and his uncle have a conversation about secrets? Andrew knew exactly what Freddie was thinking and he asked permission from his uncle to tell Freddie the circumstances of his confession. Sam nodded. "Of course," he said.

"I'll tell you about it the next time we are alone. I promise," Andrew said to Freddie and Freddie was satisfied. *Christ, we're reading each other's minds,* Andrew thought. Then he said, "I'm sorry we interrupted you Uncle Sam. You were about to spill a big secret, and I for one am waiting impatiently."

"Me too," Freddie echoed.

Sam looked at Jean and beckoned him to come and stand next to him. When Jean was at his side, the two men smiled at each other. They embraced and began to kiss each other as passionately as Freddie and Andrew had. Freddie and Andrew dropped their jaws.

"This is my secret," Sam said. "Jean and I have been lovers since we were nineteen."

"Nineteen?" Andrew asked incredulously. "I never suspected a thing. It certainly was a secret. Why are you coming out now?"

"In the beginning, I was afraid that if my enemies knew I was gay, they would find me weak, so Jean agreed to go along with this charade because he loves me. Our enemies, if any, are few now, and they know that both of you are gay. They will still fear our family because it is stronger than ever. I have nothing to hide anymore. Freddie you live here again. It was easy to be discreet when you were a kid, but it's harder to sneak around now. I don't want to have to be a sneak anymore regardless. When I am out in public now, I want Jean at my side. I don't want him dropping me off somewhere and sneaking away." Sam started to cry and he hugged Jean harder.

"I always hated that you were alone surrounded by fawning yes men, Uncle Sam. I for one could not be more pleased," Andrew stated emphatically. "Jean, thank you for taking such good care of my uncle." He kissed Jean on the lips. "And you, you old coot," he said to Sam, "no wonder you were so cool when Freddie and I came out."

Sam turned to Freddie. "Have you nothing to say to me? Are you mad at me or ashamed?"

"Oh God, no, Unc. I'm just too shocked to say anything. I'm leaving it to Andrew to speak for both of us. He's the mouthpiece here."

"It's been an exceptionally long and rewarding day, Sam said or rather sighed. "I think Jean and I will go get ready for dinner. It's too late for you to go home, Andrew. I'm sure that Freddie can give you something of Scott's to wear. You're about the same size. Why don't you two go upstairs and get ready?"

When they entered Freddie's room, they looked at each other and the lust they had experienced a little while back overtook them again. They fell into each other's arms and kissed wildly. They began to feel their hardening packages, and Freddie started to pull off his tee shirt.

"Kyle and I have an agreement," Andrew said. "We allow each other to have sex with anyone we want to, but we have to tell the other. So far it hasn't happened."

Freddie started to laugh. Scott and I never deluded one another that we could ever change our ways, and we have the same agreement, so let's stop talking and do the deed. Oh, Andrew I love you so much. If Scott left, I could survive, but if I lost you, my life would be over."

They stripped quickly and lay down on Freddie's bed. They got into a 69 position and began to play. The enormity of what they were doing, after so many, many years, excited them both beyond measure. Every stroke of Andrew's tongue sent shivers through Freddie, and Andrew was experiencing the same reaction. They both came much too quickly and each hungrily swallowed each other's juices. Afterward, they lay on the bed holding each other and kissing, and Andrew told Freddie the whole story of Joey and Carl, and how they were rescued, and how the twins were dispatched without a trace.

"I knew Uncle Sam was involved and the twins had somehow crossed him," Andrew continued the story "but I said nothing. I couldn't bear to hold the secret I held, and one day I told him. It only brought us closer together. Sam saved my life and you didn't lose me."

"They really raped you and Kyle?" Freddie asked. "If I was there and I knew about it, I would have killed them myself."

They showered together and while they were dressing, Freddie asked, "What do you make of Jean and Uncle Sam?"

"For me, that was the highlight of the afternoon. It sort of put the excitement of being a millionaire on the back burner. If you think about it Bro, Uncle Sam is in his forties and I have never known him to have a relationship with a woman. That should have told us something. So much for gaydar."

Freddie laughed. "Don't tell anyone that our gaydar failed or they'll revoke our membership in the gay club."

Just then, there was a knock at the door. Freddie was still naked, but he opened it and there stood Jean. He was dressed to the nines. Freddie and Andrew grabbed him and started kissing and hugging him. Jean was giggling like a school girl. "Careful, careful men or I'll cum in my pants."

"Thank you for your loyalty," Andrew said.

"No need to thank me. I'm family too."

When they got to the restaurant, they found Kyle and Scott at the bar. They had shared a cab from school. Sam was in an exuberant and kissy mood. He grabbed both of them and showered them with kisses on the mouth as well as their cheeks. Scott noted that Jean was to be in the celebration party and that he was not wearing his chauffer's uniform. He was not surprised at all. After all, he had a little secret. On the other hand, Kyle could not help but wonder about it.

Kyle and Scott took their drinks to the table and the others ordered drinks after they were seated. Freddie told the waiter not to come over and ask if they wanted anything. He said he would call when they needed him. He looked at his uncle and said, "I think you have something to tell Kyle and Scott, Uncle Sam, don't you?"

"Oh for sure," Sam said. "Raise your glasses gents. Drink a toast to the fact that you are both married to multi-millionaires." Kyle and Scott already knew that, and Scott joked, "I sure hope I don't get kidnapped for ransom."

That was no joke to Sam, and he said very seriously, "That's what I pay the Rodriguez cousins to prevent."

When Scott saw how disturbed and how serious Sam was he vowed to himself not to make any more jokes about being wealthy.

'Not that, Unc. The other thing," Freddie urged.

"I told Freddie and Andrew about us, darling," Sam said to Jean. "You tell Scott and Kyle."

Jean went a step further than Sam. He told the men how Sam hired him thinking he was a female prostitute. When he showed up, Sam decided it might be fun to have a go at it. "I don't have to tell you guys what an eye opener it was for Sam. He admitted to me that no woman had ever satisfied him like I did. He called me back repeatedly and eventually insisted that I give up all my other trade. I had already done that after my first night with Sam. I fell in love with him the first moment I saw him."

"I did too," Sam added, "but it was such a shock to find out that I was gay, that I couldn't admit right away, how much I loved the man. We were not yet twenty when we committed. We made up the whole man servant scenario so my enemies would not think that I was some weakling faggot. They know me and fear me now, and so Jean and I have nothing to hide anymore."

Scott made another silent vow, never to admit that he knew about them before this evening. He and Kyle jumped up and kissed Sam and Jean on the lips. "So we have many things to celebrate tonight," Kyle said. "How wonderful."

"Hey," Scott said to Andrew, "that outfit you're wearing looks familiar."

"It ought to. It's yours," Andrew said.

"Keep it," Scott said. It looks better on you than on me."

The celebration continued far after the restaurant was officially closed. Sam slipped generous tips to the bartender and the waiter before they went home. The family was actually the only occupants of the restaurant when Jean suggested they call it a night and everyone agreed.

Sam insisted, and nobody dared argue with him, that Kyle and Andrew come home with them and use the guest room this night. He didn't want them using a cab this late at night, or rather this early in the morning.

When they got home, Jean and Sam went into Sam's bedroom (actually their bedroom) and Kyle and Andrew, Scott and Freddie helped each other climb up the stairs. None of them was too steady on his feet. At the top of the stairs, Kyle and Andrew stood in front of the guest room door and Scott and Freddie stood in front of their bedroom.

"Before we go to bed," Andrew slurred, "Freddie and I have something to tell you guys."

"We have something to tell you also."

"Me first!" Andrew insisted. "Freddie and I celebrated earlier than at dinner. After the papers were signed, we made love to each other. No regrets. I love you more than ever Kyle, but I have loved Freddie all my life."

"Same thing goes for me, Scott," Freddie whined. "I hope you both understand."

"Now what did you want to tell us?" Andrew asked.

Scott and Kyle broke out laughing.

Kyle's last class ended at 4 PM. When the class was over, he went to his office and checked his messages. There was one call from Freddie telling him to meet at his restaurant at 7 PM for one huge celebration. Kyle checked his appointment book and saw that he had no student appointments that afternoon. So he walked over to Scott's office.

Scott confirmed that he had received the same message from Freddie. "It doesn't pay to go home so let's hang out here. We can get to the restaurant early and have a couple at the bar."

"Good idea," Kyle agreed.

Scott was sitting behind his desk. He stood up and walked over to the chair that Kyle was sitting in. He stood behind the chair and started to massage Kyle's shoulders.

"Ummmm." Kyle said. "That feels so good."

"I gotta tell you Kyle," Scott said. "Ever since we had that one night together, I have never stopped wanting to make love to you. Freddie and I have given each other carte blanche to be with other guys. The only requirement is that we tell each other afterwards."

"That's funny," Kyle said. "Andrew has told me more than once that I could play with you so long as I told him about it."

Scott's hand began to wander down Kyle's chest and came to rest on Kyle's package. Kyle stood up and faced Scott. Their lips met and they kissed each other lustfully. Scott locked the office door, and shut off all the lights and computers so that it seemed that the office was deserted. In minutes, they were naked and lying on the floor kissing madly. They twisted into a 69 position, and proceeded to give each other as much pleasure as they could. It was only an hour later that their partners did the same.

When they had both cum, they pressed their bodies together. They fondled each other and continued kissing until it was time to go, and take a cab to Freddie's restaurant.

"What are you guys laughing at?" Freddie asked.

"We would like to confess that we did the same thing this afternoon."

"Shit," Freddie said. He opened his arms and asked for a group hug.

"Let's face it," Andrew added. "We all love each other and why should we not show each other how much we do. If I wasn't so drunk and so tired, I'd suggest playing switch tonight, but all I want to do right now is go to bed. Kyle, honey, please get me into a bed before I collapse."

That effectively ended the night of celebration.

Over the next few months, Freddie spent very little time at the restaurant. Andrew hated to do it, but he left his firm to spend full time 'lawyering' all the family holdings. They rented a suite of offices in the same building as Andrew's old firm. When the work was overwhelming, Andrew farmed out some of his load to his old colleagues with whom he remained good friends.

CHAPTER EIGHT

On the occasion of the first anniversary of the day that the two heirs apparent to the Gardini family fortune ascended to the throne, Sam Gardini made arrangements for the three of them to have lunch at Freddie's Surf and Turf. They sat in a quiet corner of the restaurant, and after their lunches were delivered, Sam asked the waiter not to interrupt them.

"My boys," Sam said as he cleared his throat. "I am aware that it's no secret to either of you, that I have certain enterprises which I have not mentioned to you, nor do I intend to turn over to you." Two men at the table sighed inwardly with relief. "Over the past few months I have been deciding how I should best divest myself of these enterprises and to whom.

"I have three main businesses. The first of these are escort services for men, women and same sex devotees. Some people would call it a prostitution ring, but believe me; I provide only the highest class and cleanest escorts you'll find anywhere. My clients consist of some very highly placed individuals. You'd be surprised if you knew some of the men using same sex services. Hypocrisy prevails.

"The second of my enterprises is gambling. I deal in sporting events, dog and horse racing, numbers, and whatever else people want to bet on. Finally boys, and this is big, I have been involved in drug trafficking. I'm not proud of all this, but these businesses provided me with great wealth, and the ability to provide an empire of legitimate businesses, which I could pass on to you two boys. You know how much I love you both, but as lucrative as the three illegal businesses are, I don't want you to get involved.

"Over the past few months, I have made my decision and chosen my successors, but I wanted to give you boys the chance to talk among yourselves and decide if maybe you do want any or all of these businesses. If you don't, I know exactly whom I will appoint to take over each of the enterprises. I don't even want any buyout money. I have more than I need for the rest of my life and so do my two heirs."

"Uncle Sam," Freddie began, "Andrew and I have talked about this for months. We have rehearsed every script in the book practicing how to say no to you without hurting your feelings. You have made us both very wealthy men, and we are more than grateful and fully satisfied."

"Frankly, Uncle Sam," Andrew added, "I'll rest easier when you are out of it also. Please move as quickly as possible divesting yourself."

"I was sure of how you would react," Sam said, "but I needed to give you the opportunity to say no."

"You're only 45 Uncle. What will you and Uncle Jean do?" Freddie asked.

"Well, we're going to do a lot of travel, and when that's out of our system, we'll buy a place in some resort area like Boca or Scottsdale. We'll winter there and summer in New York. Maybe we'll buy something near your folks in Florida, Andrew."

"They'd like that, I know."

When lunch was over, Sam went home, and Andrew and Freddie returned to their office. "I can't work," Freddie announced when they arrived. "I'm just too happy. Let's take the afternoon off and go to my place to celebrate." Andrew did not have to be asked twice.

When they arrived at the Town House, Jean and Sam did not seem to be around, but Andrew pointed at Sam's bedroom door. It was closed and the sounds emanating from the bedroom were unmistakable. The two men smiled at each other.

"Are you thinking what I'm thinking?" Andrew asked.

"You bet I am Bro."

They stripped rapidly and then on the count of one, two, three, they burst into the bedroom, and right into Sam's massive bed and on top of the two men occupying the bed. They scared the shit out of Sam and Jean, but as soon as they realized what was happening, they burst out laughing and grabbed Andrew and Freddie in a bear hug.

They romped on the bed like four kids at sleep-away camp. Everybody tasted everybody. Everybody fucked everybody. Everybody came one way or the other. All the while, they laughed and giggled and carried on like school boys. As if that wasn't enough, while the games were going on, Scott came home. He saw the clothing lying in a heap in front of Sam's open bedroom door and immediately joined in the fun.

"This isn't fair," Andrew said. He reached for the telephone on Sam's night table and caught Kyle just coming in their front door. "Run right over to Sam's," he ordered. "You'll never guess."

Hours later, when they were all totally exhausted, Jean finally got up and announced he would make dinner for all. "Wait a minute, Jean honey," Sam said. With tears in his eyes he said, "You are all my family. I love you more than my life itself. Please take care of each other. Don't let anything happen to any of you. I couldn't bear it if any of you were harmed in any way."

All of them fell over each other trying to kiss Sam.

Six months later, Sam was fully divested of all his holdings except the 4% of the businesses owned jointly by Freddie and Andrew. He and Jean spent almost a week working with a travel agent. They customized a world tour, which would last ten months. Their trip would allow them to visit and spend substantial time in all the major cities around the world.

Without the stress of overseeing so many business enterprises, Sam was a new man. He looked years younger than his 46 years, and to Jean's delight performed better in bed. Anytime the two of them made love, which was often, you could have filmed them for a hot sequence in a porn film.

During the months that Sam and Jean were on their travels, Kyle and Andrew virtually moved into the Town House. It was convenient for Kyle and Scott to go to work together, and the same was true for Andrew and Freddie. It was also convenient when the four wanted to switch partners or have a foursome, which was also a frequent occurrence. Besides being convenient for work and sex, it was convenient when they went to sports events and theater. They would have dinner out and come home late, but always together in one cab. Of course, they had sky box seats for the Jets games. They cheered Mike and the team along, and often bet heavily on the game with Sam's successor gambling organization, headed by Joe Mariano. Joe often joined them in the sky box, and when he said, "Good night" he always added. "Don't forget guys, if you ever have a problem and need my help, just holler." None of them doubted the meaning of those words of protection.

Sam continued to pay the Rodriguez cousins to "look after" his brood. Of course, it was easier than ever for them, because the men they needed to protect were together most of the time now. Manuel and Jorge were becoming a fixture in the family also, and they two were often invited to share the sky box. They rarely hid in the background anymore, but remained close by their charges.

The spring semester was nearing an end, and Scott had successfully staffed the summer courses so that neither he nor Kyle had to teach. The four men began to discuss taking some much needed vacation time. Ideally, they would have preferred to go somewhere together, but Freddie and Andrew felt that at least one of them needed to be around to handle the businesses.

There was no doubt that Andrew and Kyle wished to spend a little time at Kyle's secluded cabin. "When we come back," they told Scott and Freddie, "you guys should use the place for a while. You'll love it there."

"If we can arrange it," Kyle said, "we can use it all summer long on alternate weeks" Kyle described the isolated setting of the cabin on a tiny inlet. "As isolated as it is," Kyle continued, "a short car ride will take you to all the amenities you might need. It's too bad it isn't big enough for all of us, even for a weekend, but surely we can manage a weekend together."

"That's for sure. If we set up some cots in the living room, or use sleeping bags, we might be able to arrange that," Andrew said.

"What about Jorge and Manuel? We'll have to give them time off. There's just no room for them, Kyle said.

"When we go separately, the couple at home will keep one of them busy in the city and the other Rodriguez can do his thing in the country," Scott advised.

So they agreed that they would alternate weeks, but would spend weekends together at the cabin, during July and August.

That year Independence Day fell on a Saturday. Andrew's sister, Sharon, and her husband invited everyone to a barbeque at their house on that day. Also invited were Mike and his family. Kyle's parents would be visiting from Rochester and they were invited also, along with Andrew's parents who were in New York for the summer. On Sunday, Mike reciprocated with the same guest list. On both days, the body guards parked discreetly one block away. Andrew and Kyle agreed to leave for the cabin on Monday morning and Freddie and Scott would come Friday evening to use the cabin the following week. Whatever the four of them planned for the weekend was up for grabs.

The back yard barbeques were very nice, but Andrew and Kyle could not wait to return to the little cabin where they fell in love and where they first made love. The Carl, Joey debacle did not taint their desires one bit. Neither of them could sleep Sunday night so they got up about three in the morning, packed their car with clothes and food, and headed for the George Washington Bridge and out of the hot, humid city.

It was such a pleasure for them to just do nothing and laze around all day. They slept late, sun bathed nude along the lake shore, made simple dinners at home, and made lots and lots of love. They spoke to Freddie and Scott every day to make sure that all was well.

They were fully aware that Jorge remained in the city, and that Manuel had driven upstate in a camper, but they never saw him. All four of them had argued with Sam that the Rodriguez cousins were no longer necessary, but he disagreed. "People as wealthy as you are need to be protected," he argued.

"So what about you and Jean?" Andrew countered.

Sam smiled and said, "We are being taken care of." Obviously they had bodyguards too, but none of Sam's heirs had ever been aware of them. *They must be awfully discreet,* Andrew thought.

Occasionally a small canoe wandered into the inlet and moored at their dock. They would then load the boat on Kyle's car racks and bring it and the exhausted boater back to Waterfall Lodge. When that happened they always had lunch or dinner at the lodge and spent some time chatting with James Harper. They found out that he had a partner and the four of them had dinner together every so often. When their week was up they reluctantly returned to the city on Sunday in the late afternoon.

The weekends were an even greater joy. The four brothers had the bed and two sleeping bags at their disposal. They drew lots for who would use the bed on Friday night. The couple remaining at the cabin for the following week then got the bed for Saturday night. They found it very exciting not knowing who would sleep with whom on Friday night, and that kept their love lives interesting and exciting.

The summer passed way too quickly, but they all agreed it was the greatest summer ever, and they couldn't wait to repeat it the following year. Andrew's parents used the cabin during the first two weeks of September, but it got too cold after that to use it any later in the season. It was not unusual to see snow in October at these high elevations.

Sam and Jean returned home from their world tour two weeks before Christmas. Andrew and Kyle began to realize that after spending an evening together with the family, they were reluctant to return to their apartment even though it was minutes away. Often they would just stay overnight in the second bedroom adjacent to Freddie and Scott.

One day Kyle observed that they had more clothing and personal stuff at the Town House than at their apartment. They also got notice that the rent on their apartment was going up another 5% on January 1.

"Why don't you guys just move in here," Freddie said. "It makes perfect sense. You're here more than there anyhow."

"Nothing would give me more pleasure," Sam added.

"I don't know," Andrew mused. "I grew up in that apartment. I'm attached in a way. Still, I must admit, it does make sense." He started to laugh. "It would make life a lot simpler for Jorge and Manuel." So the decision was made.

They contributed most of their furniture to Sam's favorite charity for abused and battered children. Once again, Kyle's books were the heaviest and hardest things to move. When they realized that he and Scott had many of the same books, they donated the duplicates to the CCNY library.

By the Easter school break, everyone was settled in and the family fell into a boring routine of domesticity.

Freddie and Andrew returned to work on the Monday morning after Easter, April 20. Kyle and Scott had another week off before having to resume their duties. At approximately 3 PM on that first Monday back, Andrew got a call from Manuel and Freddie got a call from Jorge. They both received the same message.

"Your Uncle Sam wants to see you on a matter of great urgency. You'll find his car in front of your office building. Come right down and we'll drive you right over."

Freddie rushed over to Andrew's office. "Whatever do you suppose?" he asked, sounding very concerned.

"I don't know," Andrew said, "but let's hurry."

When they ran out of the building, they saw Jorge and Manuel standing at the door of Sam's limo. They started toward the rear seats, but suddenly each of them felt something jabbing them in the chest. The object felt very much like the muzzle of a gun.

"Don't argue and don't do anything you'll regret. Our friends already have Scott and Kyle. If you don't do exactly as you are told, I'll make a little call, and you'll both be widowers. Now both of you get in the front seat and put on your seat belts," Manuel said.

He and Jorge made sure that the two men were seated in the front with seat belts securely fastened. They closed the doors and they climbed in the back. Now they exposed their guns and pointed them at the back of the heads of both their prey.

"Drive to Kyle's cabin," Manuel said to Andrew who was behind the wheel. "Drive carefully. Do nothing to arouse suspicion. If we are stopped for any reason, your fag boyfriends are goners. Do you understand?" Andrew nodded and started the car. He entered the ongoing traffic cautiously, and headed up town toward the George Washington Bridge.

This can't be happening again, Andrew thought. *Uncle Sam was right. He had always told all of them that you could trust nobody except your own family, and even then you had to keep your eyes and ears open. How stupid I am. If Uncle Sam wanted me, he would have called me himself.*

Luis and Marco Rodriguez were brothers. They were lucky enough to get out of Cuba, with their pregnant wives, literally hours before Fidel Castro marched into Havana. He marched in arrogantly, amidst cheering throngs, who believed that he was about to bestow upon them the freedoms they so desperately sought. It wasn't long before all their hopes were severely shattered, and boatloads of refugees headed out daily into dangerous waters toward the shores of Florida.

When the Rodriguez family arrived in New York, they were granted political asylum and in time, they became American citizens. Luis and Marco had difficulty mastering the English tongue and in time, they just stopped trying. This made it difficult for them, to find employment. When their wives gave birth to Jorge and Manuel, just days apart, Luis and Marco were unable to meet the bills. They feared that they would be unable to feed their infants and their wives so they began to rob little mama, poppa retail stores with great frequency. The police had bigger fish to fry, and for all intents and purposes, the two brothers had carte blanche to continue making a living the best way they knew how.

One day the brothers heard about a mob boss named Louie Gardini. He could always use good men to work in his various enterprises. Rumor had it that he paid well and was benevolent to his employees as long as they toed the line. Luis and Marco lived in fear that they would someday be caught and sent to prison. Their families would be destitute without any means of support. They decided to seek out Louie Gardini who might well be their great benefactor.

Word reached Louie that two brothers were seeking employment with him, and he agreed to meet them. The brothers were awe struck when they entered Louie's Town House. They had never seen such wealth and such luxury in their entire lives. They sat in the foyer until a good looking young man took them into Louie's office.

Louie took one look at the brothers and knew exactly what he would do with them. They were monsters, at least six and a half feet tall. Their biceps were so huge and muscular, Louie wondered if he would be able to get a tape measure around it. He immediately offered them the job of being his personal bodyguard and that included protecting his wife and young daughter and son. When he told them what their salary would be, they grabbed at the opportunity.

Unfortunately, their jobs required that at least one of them be available at all times to look after Louie's wife and children, and the other had to be totally available for Louie. Their wives didn't complain at all. They were living luxuriously compared to the old days. Unfortunately their sons, Jorge and Manuel grew up without a father and their mothers didn't much care what the boys did as long as they didn't bother them. They got in with the wrong crowd and took to stealing, as their father's had done before them. Unfortunately they were apprehended and were rewarded with prison time for their efforts.

While the boys were in prison, Louie and his wife mysteriously disappeared. Luis was following their car and he never saw it disappear from his view. One moment it was there and the next moment it was gone. Shortly thereafter

Luis was fatally shot in a back alley by an unknown assailant. Marco had not been with him when Sam's parents disappeared. He had been looking after Sam himself. Nevertheless, a few days after his brother's untimely demise, Marco befell the same fate. It should be noted that Sam had nothing to do with their deaths. At the young age of fifteen, he had enough to do just taking over and running the business. He had to assert a firm hand and prove that he was a force to be reckoned with. The Rodriguez brothers were taken care of by Louie's close personal friends, who were now looking after Sam.

When they got out of prison, Jorge and Manuel could not find employment, and so they went to see Sam Gardini. They persuaded Sam, who was not yet nineteen, to please give them their fathers' old jobs. Neither Sam nor they believed that the Rodriguez brothers had anything to do with the deaths of Sam's parents. Sam had always been fond of the Rodriguez brothers. As far as he was concerned, they were gentle giants. Also he was planning on receiving guardianship of his nephew Freddie, and wanted to make sure that the boy would be protected. Against the objection of some of his father's old friends, he gave them the jobs.

Their first assignment was exceptionally well handled. The cousins dispatched Sam's sister and her husband. The deed was quick and clean and made to look like an accident. Sam gave them a healthy bonus and for twenty six years they served him loyally until this moment in time when greed ruled their better judgment.

Nobody in the car spoke a word. Finally, when they were out of heavy traffic, and cruising at a safe 55 on The Palisades Parkway, Freddie ventured to ask, "What's this all about men? What do you hope to gain from kidnapping us?"

"About ten million bucks for each of you," Manuel answered, and the two cousins burst out laughing.

"You know how easy it is for my uncle to find you, don't you?" Andrew asked.

"Wake up! Those days are over. Your uncle is a simple private citizen now. He has lost most of his contacts. He'll fork over the money. You'll see," Jorge sneered.

The Rodriguezes had lied to make the abduction easier. Kyle and Scott were safe and unharmed. Sam and Jean were out for the afternoon and Scott and Kyle were in the library of their home, vegging out and reading. Sam and Jean came home about 4:45 PM. They were laughing and in a very good mood.

Jean immediately went into the kitchen to start dinner and Kyle jumped up to help him. Scott and Sam had been trying to out do each other in cribbage for weeks, and Sam was in the lead by thousands of points. Scott immediately got out the cards, and the ever handy cribbage board. He insisted that Sam give him a chance to come even while dinner was being prepared. They were all being super domestic while Andrew and Freddie were driving upstate with guns aimed at their heads.

At this time of year, The Waterfall Lodge was open, but attracted few visitors. During the winter season, when the snow would begin to blanket the area, they would get a good many loyal skiers who came more for the solitude, and the lodge amenities, than the skiing. But the snows had now melted and it was too cold for the summer crowd. It was unlikely that a stray canoe would find its way to the inlet.

The cabin had no heat and when the four men entered, it was very chilly and very dark. The utilities had been turned off so there was no chance of turning on the stove to get a bit of warmth. While Jorge held his gun on Andrew and Freddie, Manuel searched the cabin by moonlight and found some blankets. "This will help keep us warm," he said to Jorge as he tossed him a blanket.

The Rodriguez cousins were better prepared than the Barkin twins. They had brought along some solid rope. They tied their captives' hands behind their backs and shoved them roughly on to the sofa in the living room.

"This is exactly as we found you last time, Andrew. You're luckier this time. You have clothes on and only your hands are tied. I hope you will express your gratitude by doing to us what you did to Joey and Carl," Manuel said.

"You can kill me first," Freddie snarled. His efforts were rewarded by a slap across his face.

"Sorry buddy, you're worth more to me alive than dead, so if you don't want to get hurt, you'll do exactly as I tell you. Is that clear?" Freddie did not so much as nod his head nor blink his eyes. He just stared Manuel down and eventually Manuel turned away.

Manuel hated being defeated that way and he blurted out for no reason and certainly without any thought, "You think your fucking faggot uncle is so great, and that he's your all time guardian angel and benefactor, well think again. He's the one who had your father and mother bumped off for stealing from him. Can you imagine? He killed his own sister? What kind of monster does a thing like that? And if you think I'm lying, think again. Jorge and I took care of it for him. Some uncle you've got."

Freddie and Andrew were struck dumb. Surely Manuel was lying, just as he had lied to Uncle Sam all these years, making Sam believe in his loyalty. There was a terrible silence in the cabin and finally Freddie screamed out, "You got that backwards, you scum. Ask instead what kind of sister steals from her brother? It was my mother and father who broke the family trust. Uncle Sam was forced to do what he had to do. I can tell you that he's no monster."

"Whatever!" Manuel groaned.

Andrew wasn't sure he could accept what Freddie had just said, but in the end, he knew he would forgive Sam. He loved him too much not to. Sam did what he had to do, and Andrew knew in his heart that Sam had it in him to kill these two lying scum bags, just as he had Carl and Joey.

Jorge stared at his watch. "It's just past six," he said. "They should be starting to miss you about now. At precisely seven o'clock, when they are really beginning to panic, a courier will arrive at Sam's front door. He will deliver explicit instructions for your ransom. I would love to be a fly on the wall and see their expressions when they read the ransom note."

"What do you mean, they? I thought you had Kyle and Scott also," Andrew said.

"So sorry, you fucking pampered little piece of shit, but we lied so that you wouldn't resist us. Your faggot lovers will be as panicky as Sam," Jorge began to laugh hysterically.

"We told Uncle Sam to fire you two fat pigs a long time ago," Freddie blurted out. He received another slap across his face.

"I told you to keep your fucking mouth shut," Manuel yelled at him. Freddie began to stare him down again, which made Manuel distinctly uncomfortable.

"Enough bullshit," Jorge said. "We are still being paid to protect you two, so if you don't want anyone to rough you up, you'll give your good friends, Jorge and Manuel, a nice erotic blow job. If you try anything funny, we won't kill you but we'll cut up your faces until you look like freaks, so I'm asking you in a nice way to cooperate."

With that, he dropped his pants and undershorts to reveal a good hard erection. He grabbed his cock and waved it at Andrew. *He's not circumcised,* Andrew thought. *I hope he's cleaner than Joey Barkin.* It was so dark in the cabin that he couldn't be sure. It turned out that he was clean. That would make doing what he had to do a lot easier.

"I just wanna watch before I get mine," Manuel said. "You watch too," he said, turning Freddie's head toward Jorge's cock which was advancing on Andrew.

Andrew instinctively cringed and moved further against the sofa's arm rest. Suddenly, instead of feeling only the soft pillow, he felt something solid and very hard. It only took him a second to wonder at that. God bless an oversight! He and Kyle had never removed the knives they had hidden between the pillows and the arm rests when the Barkins had invaded their home. How in the world could he convey that information to Freddie and not alert his captors?

"After you two bozos give us the best blow jobs you have ever given in your lives, we are going to take a little ride. By then Sam will have received our note. He won't pay a dime unless he knows you dudes are alive. There's no cell phone reception here, and no phone service, so we are going to ride to the nearest town and call him and you two are going to urge him to pay the ransom or it's curtains for the two of you," Jorge advised them.

Andrew borrowed a page from Kyle's acting book. He started to laugh. "You clowns will never get a proper blow job. You are making the same mistake that the Barkin twins did. A blow job doesn't come only with mouth and tongue movement. I need to have my hands free so that I can play with your balls and your tits. If I don't do that, you aren't getting the full whammy, and your orgasm will be unsatisfying." Both Jorge and Manuel had gotten enough blow jobs from men in prison and from women at home to know that Andrew was speaking the truth.

"OK," Jorge said, "but remember, Manuel is watching us, and we have our guns pointing at both of you."

"You might as well untie Freddie too," Andrew said. "I guarantee that when Manuel gets a peek at the action, he won't be able to hold out."

"You guys win, but no funny business," Jorge said. "Manuel untie them."

As soon as they were untied, Andrew said to Freddie, "Please Bro, I need lots of room when I'm working a blow job. Move as far to the end of the sofa as possible."

Freddie thought that Andrew was losing it, but he did as he requested and then he too felt the hard object. Gingerly his fingers explored the source of the hardness. He glanced at Andrew and said, "OK Andrew, I'm with you now. Let's show these guys what a great cock sucker you are. Manuel and I are watching. His hand firmly held the handle of the steak knife.

"No matter how hard Manuel begs you, don't do a thing to him until Jorge starts to cum," Andrew advised Freddie. "I want him to see and experience his cousin getting the ultimate pleasure." Jorge grinned broadly at Andrew.

"I love how much you fags like to give head," he said.

By 5:30 PM, the Gardini household wondered why Freddie and Andrew weren't home yet. By 5:45, Sam placed a call to Andrew's cell phone. He was directed to voice mail. He got the same results when he called Freddie. Now he was really worried. His next call was to Manuel Rodriguez. Again, he was transferred to voice mail. When he called Jorge Rodriguez, he got similar results.

By 6 PM, they were all in a panic. Kyle called Andrew's secretary at home. She informed him that both Andrew and Freddie had received calls in midafternoon and had run out of the office, saying that they wouldn't be back today. She said that Andrew's caller said only that he was Manuel.

Scott called Freddie's secretary and got the same story, except that Freddie's caller identified himself as Jorge. She also told Scott that Freddie had wondered out loud what was so urgent that his uncle would summon him in the middle of a work day, and that he feared the worst had happened.

As soon as it was confirmed that Jorge and Manuel were involved, Sam went into his private study and made three calls, one call to each owner of the three businesses he had generously given to them. When he came out, he said. "Within minutes the make, model and license plate number of the car the Rodriguez boys are driving will be alerted to a whole network of friends and to the police. We can only pray that they are driving the car I gave them. I think that Freddie and Andrew would have become suspicious if they had tried to take them in a strange car.

They could only sit silently and pray that they would hear from the kidnappers and receive their demands quickly. The ringing of the front door bell was shrill, and it shattered the silence in the room. All four men jumped at the sound. Jean ran to open the door. A young teen ager identified himself as a delivery boy for a local courier service. He had an envelope for Sam G, which Jean signed for, and he tipped the boy generously.

Jean rushed back to the living room and ripped open the envelope. As he did so, a key fell to the floor and Scott quickly retrieved it. There was a note inside which Jean handed to Sam. Sam read the note out loud and everybody got sick.

Enclosed you will find a key to locker #237 at Penn Station. Deposit ten million dollars for each of your nephews in the locker no later than 3 PM the day after tomorrow. That should give you plenty of time to gather the twenty million. One of us will retrieve the money at 4 PM on the day after tomorrow. Whoever comes for the money will have one of your nephews with him. If all the money is there, your nephew will be released. When the one of us with the money returns to where your other nephew is captive, and we are certain that we have not been followed, we will leave, and your nephew will be safe. If we are followed, he will be as dead as us.

The note was unsigned.

Jorge removed his shorts and his trousers from around his ankles so that he could better straddle Andrew. He was now naked from the waist down.

"Take off your shirt," Andrew requested. "I want to suck your tits." Jorge had not expected Andrew to be so compliant. His anticipation of the ultimate blow job had his head spinning and he did whatever Andrew requested. Andrew told Jorge to lean over him and then he began to suckle Jorge's nipples. Jorge began to make little whining sounds, but his hold on his gun was as strong as ever. With one hand, Andrew began to fondle Jorge's balls and his other hand closed firmly on the handle of the steak knife.

"Suck my cock. Don't delay any longer," Jorge commanded Andrew as he aimed his gun to Andrew's forehead. Andrew did as he was ordered and he truly attempted to give Jorge a first class send off. As Jorge got more and more excited, Manuel began to strip. He got completely naked and ordered Freddie to get to work.

"No," Freddie said defiantly. "Andrew wants us to watch Jorge cum in his mouth and that's what we are going to do." Manuel resigned himself to a bit of voyeurism. He could afford to wait for the pleasures awaiting him. *These faggots feared for their lives,* he reasoned, *and they would do anything to stay alive, even give him the best blow job he ever got in his life*

By now Jorge had mindlessly laid his gun on the sofa next to Andrew. He wrapped his totally free hands around the back of Andrew's head, forcing himself deeper and deeper into Andrew's throat. Andrew was playing with Jorge's balls and he knew the man was close to climax. He could tell that his gun was not a threat at the moment. In fact, Andrew could have grabbed the gun instead of the knife but two things stopped him. His hand nearest the gun was playing with Jorge's balls and if he stopped fondling, Jorge might get suspicious. Also he couldn't be sure if the safety on the gun was off or on. If it was on, he was in danger of losing precious time, and being overpowered by the larger man.

Andrew could feel the cum rushing through Jorge's cock, seeking an exit. Jorge was screaming wildly. Suddenly his scream was interrupted in the middle of a wail, as a knife pierced his throat, going through his larynx and out the back of his neck. He died instantly. Andrew was covered with blood and semen.

Almost simultaneously, Freddie's knife found a home in Manuel's chest. In the near darkness, Manuel could not see what was coming at him. His eyes literally popped out of his head. He looked at Freddie in disbelief and raised his gun. It was no chore for Freddie to knock the gun out of Manuel's hands, as he fell dead to the floor.

"That'll teach you to mess with A Gardini," Freddie said to nobody in particular. That child like statement brought Andrew back to when they used to play together in the schoolyard, and in spite of the circumstances, he burst out laughing.

"What now?" Freddie asked. "We are both covered in blood and other things, and I don't know if going to the police is the right thing to do. By now this car is being sought in fifty states, Canada and Mexico. I'd be afraid to drive in it. Someone is liable to shoot it off the road. The land phone has been disconnected and the cell phones don't work here. Even the water has been turned off so we can't clean the blood and semen off the floors. I feel pretty out of touch and isolated."

"That's the whole object of this cabin as you well know. I can't imagine why they brought us here. They must have reasoned that since we owned the place, it's the last place anybody would look for us. Well, that was a big mistake," Andrew tried to rationalize.

"I know that the reception for cell phones is pretty good at The Waterfall Lodge," Andrew said. "Let's start walking down the road toward the lodge. We'll keep checking our cell phones until we have some bars and try to call home for help. I think we should use those blankets to keep warm."

They wrapped themselves in the blankets and started walking down the road toward the lodge. The road encircled the lake and they tried to stay in the shadows on the off chance that a stray car came along. They needn't have worried. About halfway to their destination, Andrew announced that he had two bars.

"Let's wait for three bars to be safe," Freddie advised. Almost three quarters of the way to the lodge and 45 minutes later, Freddie announced that he had three bars and he promptly called home. Jean picked up on the first ring. He was drying a wine glass when he heard Freddie's voice. He dropped the glass and it shattered all over the kitchen floor. The others came running.

"Andrew has to speak to Uncle Sam," Freddie informed Jean. "It's really important. He'll be able to tell us what to do." Freddie handed the phone to Andrew.

"Jean's on the phone," Freddie said as he handed the phone to Andrew.

"Uncle Jean," Andrew said. We are both safe and we're out of danger, but I must speak to Uncle Sam."

There was a short wait and then Andrew heard Sam bawling into the phone. "Oh my God! Are you both all right? Tell me that everything is OK."

"We are fine, no kidding, Uncle Sam, but please listen to me carefully. Freddie and I have dispatched the Rodriguez cousins. They no longer exist. But we are both covered with blood and we can't be seen anywhere."

"Good heavens, where are you?'

"Well, it all came down at Kyle's cabin, but the phone is disconnected and the cells don't work there so we have been walking for almost an hour until we got some cell phone reception. Please Uncle Sam, don't hold back. Tell me exactly how Manuel and Jorge disposed of Carl and Joey."

"Yes, yes, of course," Sam stammered. Manuel told me that they drove a short distance from the cabin and they noticed that there was a steep rise in the road. They looked toward the lake and could see that they were now high above the lake. It was almost a gorge. They removed the license plate and scratched off the VIN number. Then they put the bodies in the car and shoved it off the road and down the gorge. It sank so fast that they were certain also that the lake was very deep at this point."

"Thanks Uncle. That is very helpful. Do you think one of you can come and get us."

"You can't hang up yet. How…?" Sam started to ask, but Andrew interrupted him.

"Let me speak to Kyle," Andrew said. "I'll give him the short version which he'll understand and he can explain it all to you."

When Kyle got on the phone, he kept crying. "Andy, Andy, Andy" was all he could manage. "How did you get free?"

"Here's the story briefly because Freddie and I have lots of work to do and I don't have time to drag it out. Manuel and Jorge put us on the sofa and demanded blow jobs just like they had seen you and I giving to Carl and Joey. Kyle, honey, we never removed those steak knives hidden in the sofa, and while they were too high on sex to know what hit them, and while the cabin was dark for lack of electricity, I knifed Jorge in the throat and Freddie got Manuel in the chest. Please explain it all to the others, but please come and get us as soon as possible. Bring some stuff to wash up all the blood from the linoleum, will you."

"Yes, darling, as soon as possible." Kyle hung up.

Andrew told Freddie about the gorge. "We have to go back to the cabin and load the bodies into the car. Then we have to drive about a quarter mile in the other direction toward the waterfall, and we'll come to the gorge. When we get there, we'll give the Barkin twins some company."

They were elated now and picked up their pace on their return trip. They were back in the cabin in half an hour. Without bothering to pull out the knives from the bodies, they loaded the corpses into the back of the car. Before throwing their clothes in with the bodies, Andrew went through the contents of the pockets. Both men had a substantial amount of money, which he confiscated. There was nothing in the wallets, which would link them to anyone else. It appeared that they acted alone in this kidnapping. After his first experience with the Barkins, Andrew was somehow very glad about this.

They removed all forms of ID from the wallet. They removed the license plates from the car, and buried them under a tree. Then they scratched off the VIN number as Uncle Sam had reminded them to do. When this was done, they got in the car and drove it to the gorge, facing the lake. They put the car in neutral and started pushing. It rolled easily over the gorge and into the lake. They couldn't see much in the darkness, but they could hear the surge of water as the car hit the deep lake below. Without any light, they could only sense that the car was buried deep below the surface, perhaps resting on the Barkin's Plymouth.

They returned to the cabin to await the arrival of their family. They couldn't wait to get out of their blood soaked clothing. "We should have sent the mess down with the car," Freddie lamented.

"You're right," Andrew said. "We'll burn it when we get home."

They were naked now and wrapped in the blankets. Suddenly they both realized how tired they were. They went into the bedroom and huddled close together in the bed. The blankets and their bodies warmed each other, and they were both asleep in just a few minutes.

They were asleep for about two hours when Sam's limo arrived with Jean at the wheel, Sam in the passenger seat, and Kyle and Scott in the back seats. When they arrived, Jean popped the trunk and took out two water pails. He gave one each to Scott and Kyle and told them to fill them with water from the lake. He then removed a bag full of detergents and scrubbing brushes, and he and Sam went into the house with flash lights.

"Good God, what a bloody mess," Sam exclaimed.

"That's an understatement," Jean agreed, "but where are the boys?"

Sam directed the beam of his flashlight into the bedroom, and his heart warmed when he saw his two boys wrapped up in blankets and snoring lightly and peacefully. He closed the bedroom door so as not to disturb them. When Kyle and Scott came in, he shushed them so they would not wake the kidnapped duo. Kyle located a plastic garbage bag under the sink and they threw the bloody clothing Andrew and Freddie were wearing into the bag. Then they went to work cleaning up the cabin.

Kyle and Scott had to make several trips to the lake to clean and refill the pails. It didn't take long for the floors to be spotless, but Jean announced that the sofa would have to be reupholstered or replaced since one side of it was pretty well bloodied.

"This sofa may have saved two precious lives. No way am I getting rid of it. I'll have it reupholstered when I get up here this summer," Kyle announced. Everyone agreed by nodding their heads.

"I hate to wake the sleeping beauties," Sam said, "but I think we should head for home." Andrew and Freddie barely woke when they were put into the limo, and they fell asleep again as soon as they felt the gentle rolling of the car on the highway.

Jean and Sam were seated up front. As soon as Sam saw that he got good reception on his cell phone, he called his three "business associates" to let them know that they could call off the manhunt. He informed them that Andrew and Freddie had resolved the problem all by themselves, and that they would not be seeing the Rodriguez boys again.

Sam's associates were more than impressed. Word spread, and Andrew and Freddie became an esteemed legend in certain segments of New York society. Shortly thereafter, some of their enterprises had a surge of new business as Sam's associates decided that these were men they could rely on.

In the days that followed the kidnapping, the Gardini family became extra diligent. They realized that their wealth endangered their lives. They fired Sam's "discreet" bodyguards, and began to interview replacements for them and the Rodriguezes as well. They only hired men with wives and children and insisted on knowing where their families lived. It was clear to the bodyguards that if they tried anything out of the way, their families would be in danger. On Christmas Day, a representative of Sam's would drop in at each of the bodyguards' homes with generous gifts for their families. It was a subtle way of letting them know that Sam knew where their families were. The bodyguards appreciated the outpouring of gifts anyway, and their children were ecstatic. Since all the family businesses were legitimate, the bodyguards had it easy. They needn't worry about business rivals. They need only concentrate on keeping the family safe from kidnappers and extortionists.

CHAPTER NINE

When Kyle opened the cabin for summer use on Memorial Day weekend, he arranged to have the sofa reupholstered. When the workman asked how so much blood had gotten on it, Kyle answered rather sheepishly, "I'm a first class klutz and I cut myself slicing an apple." The upholsterer was satisfied.

The first chance he got, Andrew hid two butcher knives between the cushions and the arm rests of the newly upholstered sofa. He knew it was an irrational act, but it was a reflection of the fact that he was not yet over the two kidnappings he had suffered in his life. He wondered if he would ever get over it.

Kyle, Andrew, Freddie and Scott continued to share the cabin on weekends, and separately on alternate weeks, but this year Jean and Sam joined them every weekend. They stayed at the lodge, however. Sam was particularly happy to meet James Harper, who had saved his nephews' lives.

Andrew's parents used the cabin for the two weeks following Labor Day as had become their habit. Jean and Sam decided to stay at the lodge during those weeks. The four of them had dinner together every evening and Sam quizzed the Stanleys about the condo they owned in Boca Raton and about the amenities offered by the community. It sounded so wonderful, and they really didn't want to spend another frigid, snowy winter in New York. Money was not a consideration and if they wanted to go to the theater or the opera in New York, they could simply fly in for the occasion. After very little discussion, Jean and Sam decided to go down to Florida the following week to buy a condo. The Stanleys gave them a key to their place and begged them to use it since it would be vacant until the first week in October when they would drive down for the season.

Whenever any of the Gardini family travelled, or if they went in separate directions, there was always the question of what to do logistically about the four bodyguards. Sam decided that they would get a three bedroom unit. One bedroom would be for guests, like Kyle and Andrew or Scott and Freddie. The third bedroom would be for the bodyguards. They figured that they would use the condo about four months a year. They would have a body guard come down a month at a time, so each of them would have a stay in the Sunshine State during the cold winter months. The lucky guys who would be down over the Thanksgiving and Christmas holidays could invite their wives and children down and Sam would put them up at a nearby hotel. How could anybody not be happy with those arrangements?

Sam, Jean and Ron, one of the bodyguards, emerged from the terminal in Ft Lauderdale/Hollywood International Airport and they were hit by a blast of furnace like air, which seemed to be bathed in bath water. Nobody warned them that September was the hottest, most humid month of the year in South Florida. They were happy to board the air conditioned shuttle bus to take them to the car rental terminal.

Dave Stanley had written out specific directions to his condominium complex, and they arrived without one false turn. They parked in Dr. Stanley's assigned parking spot and entered the building with the keys he had given them. Their apartment was on the fifth floor on the ocean side of the building. They entered the spacious apartment and immediately turned down the thermostat to make the place cooler. They opened all the blinds to let in the sunshine and were bowled over by the spectacular view of the ocean from the living room. There was an outdoor terrace off the living room. They stepped outside and in spite of the hot, humid day, they were greeted by a delightful breeze coming at them from the ocean.

The apartment had an eat in kitchen, a dining room, living room, two bedrooms, a den and two bathrooms. The area was approximately 2000 square feet. Ron threw his bags down in the guest room and Sam and Jean claimed the master bath. The Stanley's had informed them that there was a fully equipped workout room in the basement and a huge Olympic style community pool. The terrace had a wall on each end so that it was completely private from the neighbors on each side. "Would you guys mind if I sun bathed nude on the terrace?" Ron asked.

"Not at all," Sam answered. "We'll probably join you. However, we can do better than that. A friend of mine gave me the name of a nude beach in Ft. Lauderdale. We'll be going there as often as we can, so you'll have to go too. Fortunately for us, and unfortunately for you, Ron, it's a gay beach. You can wear a swim suit if you want to."

"I can handle it. I think I'd prefer to go nude. If anyone comes on to me, I'll tell them I belong to you," Ron joked.

"Trust me," Jean said. "Plenty of guys will come on to you."

In the end, they had such a wonderful time that they extended their stay an extra week. They ended up buying a three bedroom penthouse apartment in the same building. It had just come on the market the day they arrived. They paid the asking price and said that it would be a cash deal. Talk about happy sellers.

They intended the third bedroom to be for whichever body guard would be down south with them. They furnished it with twin beds so that if any of their nephews came down, the bedroom would accommodate another bodyguard.

They found out that the area boasted two first class opera companies that could be seen in West Palm Beach and Ft. Lauderdale. They bought subscriptions to each of them. The Broward Center for the Performing Arts in Ft. Lauderdale, and the Kravis Center in West Palm Beach also showed Broadway Theater in season and there were dozens of regional theaters as well. The Miami City Ballet performed at the Broward Center. They were surprised and delighted to find that their new home was not located in a cultural wasteland, and they realized that they wouldn't have to go to New York as often as they thought. Instead, they would urge their boys to visit them as often as possible. They knew that the Stanleys would be more than pleased about that.

They went to the gay nude beach several times and earned some pretty bad sun burns for their efforts, in spite of applying sun block generously. As promised, Ron had to fend off many of the men who came on to him. Although he was forty, his body was that of an athlete, and a seven inch flaccid cock didn't hurt either.

After consulting the gay yellow pages on line, they located a gay bar in Ft. Lauderdale and they went there on the evening before they returned home. Ron stayed discreetly in a corner nursing a coke all evening. Nobody came on to him, and he admitted in the car driving back to Boca that he was a little deflated by that. On the other hand, Jean and Sam met several other couples there and they all had a great time huddled at the piano bar around the piano. They agreed to get together when they came down in November. Unfortunately they didn't have a phone number yet or cards, so Jean wrote down both their cell phone numbers on a slip of paper and handed it to one of the men. He carefully placed the cards, offered by their new friends, in his wallet.

It was with great reluctance that they drove off to the car rental return on their last morning in Florida. Ron told them that he hoped he would draw the watch for December, so that his family could join him in paradise this Christmas. Jean wished him luck. Ron had other reasons for wanting to come down again. The apartment was not so well insulated that he didn't hear Sam and Jean going at it every night. He began to wonder what it would be like to make love with a man. His wife wasn't frigid, but it took him so long to get her aroused that sometimes he lost interest by the time she was ready. A man was always ready. Besides, listening to Sam and Jean having sex got him so hot that he could only relieve himself by whacking off. There was nothing unusual about that, but he began to fantasize that he was the third party in bed with them and his reality orgasms were beyond all his expectations. If he came down south again, at the very least, he could whack off to the sounds of their love making. Subtly, by inches, he was beginning to envy gay men. When he got home and he made love to his wife, he began to visualize the nude men on the beach and the camaraderie at the gay bar. Most of the time he would shudder at his 'unnatural' yearnings, but other times he had the strongest urge to act on them.

The wives of the other three bodyguards seemed very content that their husbands were rarely home. The salaries they earned were beyond anything they had previously achieved. None of them cheated and none of them were lonely. The money and their families kept them happily satisfied. Ron's wife was different. Yes, she enjoyed her new wealthy life style, and she didn't miss Ron for the sex, but she was lonely at night when he wasn't around, which was most of the time.

Rhonda had three single divorced girlfriends, who kept urging her to go out with them. They assured her that all they ever did was to have a few innocent drinks at a local watering hole. Her two sons were now twelve and fifteen years old and required no baby sitter, so it was easy for Rhonda to get out whenever she wanted to. The first time she joined her friends, it became obvious to her that a few innocent drinks was not what they had in mind. These women were on the prowl and they were hungry for sex. Usually at least one of them hooked up for the night. One night all three scored and they disappeared so fast, it took Rhonda a little while to realize that she was alone in the bar. She decided to finish her drink and then head for home.

"Can I buy you another drink?" she heard a friendly voice ask. She turned around to see a very handsome middle age man smiling at her. Somewhere an overhead light was shining on him, making his white teeth gleam. Rhonda had to blink, the sparkle was so intense. His brown hair was gray at the temples, and his brown eyes reminded her of a puppy she had owned as a child. He was dressed as if he was ready to pose for GQ. She smiled back at him.

He held out his hand to her. "My name is Frank Mason," he said. Rhonda took his hand.

"I'm Rhonda Harte," she said. She was flattered and a little frightened. She wanted to leave and probably should have, but instead she said, "Why yes. You can buy me another drink. That would be very nice."

She didn't go home with Frank that night, but they met at the bar several times over the next few weeks. She let him know that she was married and had two teen age sons. It didn't seem to diminish his desire for her in any way. Finally one day, she told him that her boys were spending the night with their grandmother, and she agreed to go to Frank's bachelor pad. She was actually frightened, and she was prepared to feign arousal and orgasm, which she rarely achieved with Ron. She was surprised and delighted when Frank tenderly began to make love to her and she was almost instantly aroused. She didn't have to pretend anything, and she achieved orgasm three times.

She was happier than she had ever been in her life, but terribly confused. Why didn't she feel this way about Ron? She thought she loved her husband. She had never doubted it. This was her first affair, and anyway, it was his fault, wasn't it? Sometimes he wasn't home for weeks at a time. How could he expect her to live like a nun? Besides, maybe he was screwing some bimbo at the Gardini house. She made excuse after excuse, but she could not erase the perfectly clear fact, that she was madly in love with Frank Mason, and that she now realized that she had never loved Ron Harte.

It was decided by lot that Kyle and Andrew would go down to Florida for Thanksgiving and that Freddie and Scott would go down for Christmas. All of Sam's nephews would be together in New York for the New Year celebration. The four bodyguards, Ron, Ernie, Art and Mel drew lots also. One of them was assigned to each couple a month at a time. The fourth was sort of a rover. He would be around if the couples had to split or if one became ill. The rover accompanied Kyle to a conference once, and on another occasion, he accompanied Freddie to a business meeting in Chicago. Ernie was assigned to Kyle and Andrew for November, which meant that he would be in Boca Raton for Thanksgiving. Mel was already down south as he had drawn Jean and Sam for November. Sam made reservations for Ernie and Mel's families to stay at the hotel. Every other night one of the men could stay overnight at the hotel. At least one of them was required to stay at the condominium. Besides paying for the airfare of the bodyguards' families, Sam intended to give them a generous check for expenses while down south.

Mel was the oldest guard at forty-eight. His children were married and out of the house. Mel's wife decided to make Thanksgiving at home and have her children with her. She was influenced by the birth of a brand new grandson. Sam cancelled her hotel reservation, and Mel told Ernie he could stay at the hotel every night while his family was down in Florida, if he wanted to.

Ron had gotten his wish and he drew Freddie and Scott for December so he would therefore get to spend Christmas in Florida with his family. The four guards all became good friends, and were so well treated by Sam, Jean and their nephews that there was nothing they wouldn't do for them. Their bonds were sealed when on the first of January, each body guard received a brokerage statement for each of their children with an initial investment of $1000.00 each. The broker's statement was accompanied by a letter from Sam in which he informed them that he would add an additional $1000.00 at the beginning of each fiscal quarter. The money was set aside for the children's college educations. In Mel's case it was for his grandson.

Andrew and Kyle arrived on the Tuesday before Thanksgiving. Andrew's parents had driven down in October with a seven seater minivan loaded with stuff for their apartment. They, Mel, Jean and Sam drove to the airport together to pick up Andrew, Kyle, and Ernie in the van. Fortunately Ernie's wife and two kids were not coming down until the next day. Jean said that he and Mel would pick them up.

Anna Stanley was making the holiday dinner in her apartment, and Jean and Kyle were quick to insist on helping her. Andrew said that he and Kyle would stay in his parent's apartment so that Mel and Ernie could have separate bedrooms when Ernie's family was no longer at the hotel, but Sam would not allow them to be anywhere without protection. So in the end they stayed with Uncle Sam. Sam had previously and carefully explained to the Stanleys why it was necessary that Andrew have a body guard. He left out the tale of the Rodriguez cousins, but the Stanleys appreciated how wealthy their son was, and the need for him to be kept safe, just like all those Hollywood celebrities.

The minute Andrew, Kyle and Ernie were settled in, they ran down to the ocean for a swim. Sam and Jean didn't even have a chance to tell them how to get to the gay nude beach, but they vowed to take them out to dinner that evening, and to meet their new friends at the gay bar. Sam told the Stanleys what was planned for the evening and invited them to join, but they primly declined.

Bodyguard Art was assigned to Freddie and Scott for November, and Ron was the rover. When Freddie and Scott started out to work the morning after Kyle and Andrew left, Art wasn't ready to go with Freddie, but Ron, who was at home the night before, came running up the steps to go with Scott. They knocked on Art's door to see why he wasn't ready, and found him lying in bed unable to move. He had a fever of 102 and the obvious symptoms of the flu. They called a cab to take him to their doctor, and then to take him home.

Security at CCNY was very tight since 9/11 and all those school massacres around the country and the world, so it was decided that Ron would go with Freddie and Scott would go solo to work just this once. "Once you are safe in your office," Ron said, "I'll go home and get some stuff because I'm staying at the Town House tonight." Freddie started to object but Ron would not hear of it. In the cab coming home from work that evening, Ron announced to Freddie that he and Scott were going to be his guests for Thanksgiving dinner at his home, and that was not open for discussion either.

The guys were used to Jean having dinner ready every night and none of them excelled at cooking. Jean and Kyle were the only chefs around here, so they decided to go out to dinner in their absences.

"I hope you won't mind," Scott said to Ron, "our favorite restaurant is in the village. It's gay owned and operated and the food is to die for. Most of the clientele is gay." Ron felt a stirring in his groin.

"That's fine with me," he said. "You should see the places your uncles took me to, including gay nude beaches."

"Wow," Freddie exclaimed. "They never mentioned it."

At dinner that evening, all three of them were cruised. Ron had learned to recognize the signals, and he was secretly pleased and more than a little aroused. It did not get by Scott what was going on with Ron, but Freddie was totally oblivious.

"The way you are getting the eye from the guys here, Ron, I'd bet that you could go home with any one you liked; that is if you weren't straight and married," Scott observed.

"To tell the truth," Ron answered, "I'm totally flattered. You should see how I had to fight them off at the gay beach." After that the subject was dropped except that during the meal, Ron received several nods from admirers and he smiled and nodded back. Scott was taking it all in. *If he was alone he'd go home with one of them. I can feel it in my bones,* he thought.

"A penny for your thoughts, big guy," Scott said. "If you want one of those guys, I can fix it up for you."

Not only did Ron turn a deep shade of crimson, Freddie choked on his wine. Ron's first thought was to make a joke out of Scott's offer, which it probably was. Then he got to thinking. He never thought of Andrew, Kyle, Freddie or Scott as employers. Weren't they doing Thanksgiving together? As far as he was concerned, they were friends. Did he dare confide in them about his conflicted sexual feelings, which had surfaced in Florida last September, or should he just ignore the whole thing? He really didn't think it out very well when he said, "That's an interesting offer Scott. Can I talk to both of you about something?"

Freddie's brain said, "Uh oh!" and Scott said, "Talk away, Ronnie baby. I'm an excellent listener." Ron's hand was on the table and Scott placed his hand over Ron's. Ron was surprised and very titillated. He made no attempt to move his hand.

"Well guys, as you know, I often sleep in the Town House, but the house is huge and although I can hear the sounds of all you guys going at it, it's kind of distant and indistinct. I never gave it much thought. But in Dr. Stanley's condo, you can hear everything that's going on in the apartment. Going to the gay beach and visiting the gay bar with your uncles, I must admit, began to turn me on. At night I could clearly hear Jean and Sam making love. They're pretty noisy."

Freddie and Scott nodded in agreement.

"Anyway, as you can imagine, I got aroused, and I started to whack off. In the past when I whacked off, I pictured that a buxom twenty year old blond with big boobs was sucking my cock. My fist was her mouth. But listening to your uncles, I began to fantasize that one of those hunks at the beach was doing the honors. Then it got worse. I began to fantasize that I was in bed with Jean and Sam and making love to both of them."

Freddie and Scott were silent so Ron continued. "I began to wonder what it would be like to really have sex with a man, or better still, I began to wonder what it would be like to *make love* to a man. When I got home, I couldn't get excited for my wife unless I fantasized I was with one of the guys at the beach or one of your uncles." Ron was out of words and he buried his face in his hands.

Freddie carefully removed his hands and made Ron look him straight in the eye. "Believe me Ron; Scott and I know just how it is. It's a hunger you can't bury or deny. Would you be willing to have a go at it with a man? If it doesn't work for you, well that's that. We certainly won't tell on a friend. But if it works for you, I pity you. It's a hard thing to fight. You can never put it on the back burner. It'll haunt you, and you'll be forced to do it again and again in an effort to satisfy your desires."

"If you are willing to try, here are your options." Scott continued. "We can take one of these hunks home with us, but no matter how good looking he may be, there is no guarantee that he's a good lover. On the other hand, Freddie and I would be delighted to give you your first experience. Your first could very well be your last experience, and I promise we'll make it a night you will never forget. Don't answer quickly. Look around the room and think carefully.

Ron did just that. He looked around the room and concluded that Freddie and Ron were as good looking, or maybe better looking, than any guy in the restaurant. Also they had great bodies.

"If I slept with you guys, would you want me to still be your body guard?" Ron asked with real concern.

"More than before," Freddie answered. "I would think that you would want to fully protect the guys who took your virginity." That made them all laugh. "Then I choose you," Ron said.

"I hoped you would say that," Scott said.

"We can't leave yet," Ron said. "I'm splitting my pants."

The three of them lay naked and still in Freddie's king size bed. Ron was in the middle. "Are you scared?" Freddie asked Ron.

"Not in the way you think. I'm not scared of making love to a man. I'm scared to death, I'll like it too much."

"Well, we warned you," Scott said. "You can still change your mind."

"Look," Ron said, pointing at his huge hard cock. "Does this look like I want to change my mind?"

"Well then, here goes," Freddie said. He turned to Ron and placed his lips on Ron's. The bodyguard was stunned. He hadn't counted on kissing being part of the equation, but he was committed and he returned Freddie's kiss with closed lips. Freddie opened his mouth and started to part Ron's lips with his tongue. Freddie was patient. He knew what would happen and he was right. Little by little, Ron began to kiss back with passion. Of course, it helped a lot that Scott was sucking one of Ron's tits and fondling his balls while he and Freddie kissed. In a short while, Ron was kissing Freddie just like he used to kiss his wife when he was trying to get into her pants. The difference is that he wasn't fantasizing kissing his wife. He was living in the moment, content that he was kissing Freddie. He was more than content. He was happy.

"Have you ever cheated on your wife?" Scott asked out of the blue.

"Never! This is the first time, and because it's not with a woman, I don't really feel like I'm cheating. Why did you ask?"

"Then none of us has been exposed to any STD's and we can go at it without condoms. Is that OK with you?" Scott asked.

"Oh sure. My wife had her tubes tied after my last kid was born, and I haven't used a condom since."

"Good, then let's not talk so much and get on with it." Scott said.

Freddie and Scott tongued their way down each side of Ron's body. From his moans and his sighs, it was obvious that Ron was thoroughly enjoying it. When they completed their journeys south, they both ran their tongues up and down his cock and when finally Freddie engulfed Ron's massive Rod in his mouth, as best he could, Scott sucked on his balls. Ron's body was writhing. He looked like he was having a seizure.

"Oh God, oh God," he whined over and over again. Freddie felt that he was close and withdrew.

"Please don't stop," Ron begged.

"Don't worry there's more to come," Scott said. "We're going to form a daisy chain. We'll each have a cock in our mouths, and after we all cum, we are going to get some sleep. In the morning if you want to forget the whole deal, you'll take Freddie to work and we will never speak of this again. If you want more, we'll teach you more. Deal?"

"Deal!" Ron said.

"Then let me teach you how to suck cock." In his best professorial manner, Scott instructed Ron in how to use his lips and his tongue and how to tuck in his teeth. Before forming the chain, Ron was even willing to practice a little bit on each of his employers. Afterward he declared, "It really tastes very good. I didn't expect that."

Before they began the daisy chain, they allowed Ron to come down from his near high so that he wouldn't cum too fast. Finally, it was Freddie who got impatient and demanded that they get going.

"Scott and I swallow our cum," he told Ron, "but if you don't want to do that, you can spit it out."

"I'll swallow. I committed myself to go all the way."

They formed the chain and went to work. After several minutes nobody had cum, so on a whim they reconfigured the chain so that they each had a different cock to suck. After that, they came quickly one after the other. True to his promise, Ron swallowed every drop as did the others.

They washed up and Freddie turned out the lights. They fell asleep nesting against each other. Again, Ron was in the middle. He loved the way his cock nested in Freddie's crack and the way Scott's nested in his.

Just before dawn, Ron needed to pee badly, but he was in the middle. There was nothing he could do but climb over Freddie. He then headed to the bathroom. Neither of his bed mates even stirred. When he returned from the bathroom, he could only smile. Scott and Freddie had somehow found each other. They were wrapped up so tight, he could not hope to resume his middle position. He didn't bother to go back to bed. Instead he went naked into the kitchen and took out rolls and bagels from the freezer and then set up the coffee. All he had to do when they were ready for breakfast was to push the on button.

When Freddie and Scott woke up, they would want to know what decision he had come to. He was still uncertain himself, but he knew for sure that he had loved the experience and he had the time of his life. He also knew that when Scott promised to teach him more, he meant anal sex. Ron had never fucked anyone through the rear door, male or female. He had no doubt that he would love doing that. When he used to listen to Sam and Jean he could picture what act they were performing. He learned to recognize the squeals of delight when they were fucking each other. But what would happen to his male macho image if some guy fucked him? *Well*, he concluded, *it doesn't matter. I'm not making a decision until I experience everything.*

He tried to picture either Freddie or Scott fucking him. He searched his soul to see if the thought disgusted him, but he felt nothing. On the other hand, thinking of fucking them led to a rising cock. He just had to find out for himself. He returned to the bedroom. The lovers were still wrapped up together in the middle of the bed. He shook Scott's shoulder because Scott was the more aggressive lover of the two.

"Wha….what?" Scott asked.

"I want to fuck one of you and I want you to fuck me," he said and it sounded like a command to the troops. Scott disengaged himself from Freddie, and he and Ron went into the bathroom. "I gotta pee," he said and then we should brush our teeth."

While he was peeing, Freddie came into the bathroom and he and Scott crossed swords. After they washed the sleep out of their eyes and brushed their teeth, they climbed back into bed. Scott opened his night table drawer and took out a big tube of KY Jelly. "Lie on your back," he instructed

Freddie, who gladly obliged. Ron watched as Scott lubed Freddie's hole generously.

"If we had showered and we were sparkling clean, I would have rimmed my baby first to get his juices going, but we don't have much time now. If you vote for more, we'll do it better tonight," Scott told Ron.

Ron was only semi erect so Scott took his cock gently in his hand and moments later, with little effort, Ron was hard as nails. Scott then lubricated Ron's prick with the lubricant. He positioned him between Freddie's legs. Freddie moaned softly and raised his buttocks. Scott placed a pillow under Freddie's raised ass, and guided Ron's cock into Freddie's pleading ass hole.

"Aah, aah, aah," Ron could only repeat over and over as he gently began an in and out stroking motion, just as if he was fucking a vagina. Only no vagina he had ever visited was as tight as Freddie's ass, nor as moist, nor as warm. Ron had hoped he would hate this, but he loved it. He had achieved Nirvana.

Almost in a dream, he heard Scott say, "I'm going to grease us both up good, but even so this will hurt at first. Just bear it. I promise you that the hurt will turn to pure pleasure." Ron could feel Scott lubricating his ass hole. *We usually rim it after a shower;* he could hear Scott whispering earlier. *We had enough time to shower. I could kick myself,* he thought. Once or twice, Scott's massaging finger touched Ron's prostate and tears came to his eyes, tears of joy.

He was roused from his reveries when he felt Scott's cock head looking for his ass hole. "Man, you have a huge opening. This shouldn't be bad at all."

Ron was aware when Scott's medium size cock reached his muscle, and when Scott went right in it barely hurt at all.

"Did that hurt?" Scott asked, concerned.

Ron couldn't talk. He just shook his head. He resumed thrusting in and out of Freddie's ass hole and it felt heavenly. But when Scott's cock started to massage Ron's prostate, his tears returned, and he was overwhelmed with the realization that he was experiencing the full potential of his sexual being. All the rest had been practice leading to this moment. He heard Freddie yelling, "Fuck me harder, baby," and he and Scott started thrusting harder. Ron felt like he was taming a wild horse and he rode harder and harder until he came screaming like a wild man. Seconds later Freddie shot up his abdomen and chest, and Scott let loose inside of Ron.

Ron could feel the warm fluid spurting inside of him and filling him up. *What will I do when he pulls out?* Ron thought. *I'll be empty. I won't be able to stand it.*

"We better shower," he heard Scott say as he pulled out of him. Ron did indeed feel like there was a void, a mile wide canyon in his body that needed to be filled badly. They used the shower in this room and the one in Andrew's room. When they went downstairs, they found breakfast almost ready for them.

"Talk!" Scott demanded of Ron. "I gotta know."

Ron encircled Scott in a bear hug. "That was the best thing that ever happened to me in my life. I've got to have more. I need to have more so badly." He looked at Freddie, "You were right," he said. "I'm deathly afraid of my future. How can I live my old life, knowing that I am gay."

"It's going to be tough, but we'll help you," Freddie said and he embraced both Scott and Ron who were still holding each other.

"I've got to make a call," Ron said and he disentangled himself. He called Art who said he was better, but still had a low grade fever.

"Take your time getting back to work," Ron said. "I've got everything under control."

On Thanksgiving Day, Freddie and Scott gathered the flowers they had bought for Rhonda and the IPods they had bought for Ron's sons while Ron hailed a cab to take them to Thanksgiving Dinner at his house. Ron was excited, but he was a little frightened too. He wondered if there was any way that Rhonda would be able to detect that he had slept with Freddie and Scott. He finally rationalized that she could not.

When they entered his apartment, Ron had expected to smell all the wonderful odors of the traditional Thanksgiving Day feast, but there were no smells in the apartment at all. He called out for Rhonda, but received no answer. He ran first to the kitchen. It was obvious that no cooking had gone on here for quite a while. He ran into his bedroom expecting to find Rhonda's corpse on their bed, but the bed was neatly made and no bodies were visible. He looked in the closet. His clothes were intact, but all of Rhonda's were missing. From there he headed for his sons' bedroom, which they shared. The bedroom was empty; no clothes, no furniture, no sons.

Freddie and Scott could see that he was in a panic and had been following him around the apartment. "She must have left a note or something," Scott said. "Let's look." Freddie found the note on the front hall table. They had all missed it upon entering the partially empty apartment. Ron grabbed the note from Freddie and started to read out loud.

Dear Ron: I'm sorry to do this to you in such a harsh way, but I am feeling very guilty and really can't face you just now. I have fallen in love with a wonderful man, a man who will be mine 24/7. I know that you can't be there for me like he can, but I don't blame you. You are making a wonderful living now, and you must do your duty.

Frank Mason is very wealthy and I won't want any alimony from you, but I will expect child support, of course. You can visit with the boys anytime your schedule allows. I realize that we can't make a steady visitation schedule, your job being what it is.

The boys and I have moved in with Frank at 222 Park Avenue, Apartment 307. You can reach me on my cell phone anytime. I know I have hurt you and I am sorry, but I have to think of me too, and I have never been happier. And the boys have a father, at last.

I have instructed my attorney to reach you at Mr. Gardini's home.

Rhonda.

Ron slumped down on a kitchen chair and buried his head in his hands. "Are you all right?" Freddie asked with great concern.

Ron took his hands away from his face and looked up at Freddie. He was grinning from ear to ear. "Surely you realize what a load off my mind this is. Do you think one of you guys could use your influence and get us a table at a good restaurant for Thanksgiving Dinner?"

CHAPTER TEN

Art returned to work on Saturday morning, and Ron had to reprieve his role as the rover for another week until he became full time body guard to Freddie and Scott during the month of December. He couldn't wait for that day to come, of course, but there was a fly in the ointment. Kyle and Andrew were returning on the Sunday night after Thanksgiving and there would be another bodyguard in the house. As a rover, he would be sleeping at his own home unless needed. Beginning December 1, Mel would be guarding Kyle and Andrew, Ernie would be guarding Sam and Jean, and Art was the designated rover for December.

On Friday night Ron consulted with Freddie and Scott. "Should I come out to Kyle and Andrew when they get home? Should I eventually come out to Sam and Jean?"

"Yes," they answered simultaneously.

"Look guys," Ron continued. "Maybe the other guys can live celibate lives and be happy whacking off every night, but that's not good enough for me anymore. You have shown me a better way. I need to live the life you have initiated me into. Would you consider replacing me as a body guard, and giving me a job in one of your other enterprises? I need to have a home life, someone to go home to every night like you guys have."

"Yes," they answered simultaneously again. "Just give us a day or two to think about the best thing to do."

Ron thanked them and spent the night in their bed. On Saturday morning, he returned to his empty apartment. On Saturday evening, he returned to the gay restaurant where he first came out to Freddie and Scott. He ordered dinner and dined alone. This time when someone approached him, he showed interest and long before midnight, he was sharing his bed with a gorgeous hunk of a man. Ron's new life as a practicing homosexual was very much on its way.

He had a wonderful time and confirmed that he enjoyed gay sex so much more than straight sex. The downside was that Nat, his bed partner for the night, was not nearly as adept at making love as Freddie and Scott. In fact, newbie Ron showed him a thing or two.

Since taking over Sam's businesses, Andrew and Freddie had started a program of expansion. One of the new enterprises was a string of retail stores in several major cities with large gay populations. The merchandise sold in these stores was aimed at appealing to gays and lesbians. Besides provocative clothing, they sold all sorts of gay toys and paraphernalia. Each store had a manager, but with the opening of a sixth store, Andrew felt that a general manager should be hired to oversee the entire chain and monitor the managers, buyers and the sales people. Andrew asked Ron if he would consider the newly established position.

"Does a cat have nine lives?" he asked. "You bet, I will."

"I figure that you'll only have to travel one week a month unless you expand the enterprise even further. That will give you plenty of time to see your staff," Freddie added.

"If it gets big enough," Ron said, "I can foresee regional managers down the pike."

"I like the way you think," Andrew said as he put out his hand to shake Ron's.

Ron's replacement for the bodyguard position was harder to fill. They began to interview after Christmas when they returned from Florida. The first three candidates were all family men, but each said that they would not be comfortable working for fags. Oops and out. The fourth candidate was thirty-three years old, married with three kids.

"I would have no problem guarding gay men at all," John Davis said.

"You might have to go to gay establishments with them," Andrew advised.

"Been there and done that. My older brother is gay. I love him, and I am very fond of his friends. I've gone to gay bars with them on many occasions. A lot of guys have come on to me there and I've warded off plenty of their advances. Believe me. I can handle it."

"Does your brother look like you and is he single?" Andrew asked.

"Yes, to both questions. Why do you ask?"

"Have we got a guy for him," Freddie said.

"Boy, if you could get my brother to settle down, I'll give you my first week free, that is, if I'm hired," John said with a question mark in his voice.

"You're hired and it won't be necessary to give us a free week," Freddie said. "Now let's talk about something really important. How can we get your brother and Ron together?"

"Mark has a degree in accounting but he's in a dead end job with the city of New York. Maybe you have something for him?" John asked.

"Our head accountant has been screaming at me to hire an assistant for him for months. He just has too many different businesses to manage by himself. It's definitely beginning to overwhelm him. Do you think Mark would be interested in speaking to us about that job?" Freddie asked.

"I'll ask him? He'd be a jerk to pass up an opportunity like this."

Ron now had a private office in the Gardini suite of offices. Andrew arranged an interview with Mark Davis at 11 AM on a Friday morning. He thought the timing was perfect for what he had in mind.

Mark was first interviewed by Hank Morrissey, the chief accountant, and then by Freddie and Andrew. Hank, Andrew and Freddie thought that Mark would be perfect for the job. Hank particularly felt that he and Mark could work well together. Once it was established that Mark was the man, and he accepted the position, they agreed upon salary. Mark was just a few dollars shy of doubling his present salary. He said that he felt morally obligated to give two weeks notice, and he could start two weeks from Monday. Everyone said that would be just fine.

Then Andrew's plan went into high gear. Previously he had asked Ron to have lunch with him and Freddie. Well, you didn't refuse the bosses, now did you? Andrew asked Mark to come back to his office for a little chat. Mark was flattered but a little nervous.

"I'm very fond of your brother, John," Andrew began. "I feel safe in his hands, and I know I'm going to feel safe in yours; in a different way, of course. Your brother replaced a man who now works here in the office with us. His name is Ron Harte. Ron is having lunch with Freddie and me today, and I'd like for you to join us. Your brother John was assigned to me this month. Do you see that closed door over there? John is in it, seated at a bank of monitors, and watching surveillance cameras all over the office. He'll be joining us for lunch also."

"That would be great," Mark said. "I took the whole day off and I have plenty of time. In fact, I'd like to come back after lunch and maybe Hank could show me around the operation and orient me a little bit."

"Or Ron," Andrew said hopefully.

The five men assembled at the elevator to go to lunch. Ron had been clued in that Mark was gay, but Mark was not told about Ron, only because the opportunity had not presented itself. When Ron got to the elevator, he was introduced to Mark. *He's so handsome. I could really go for this guy,* Ron mused to himself. In the elevator, he stood next to Mark, and at lunch he managed to sit next to him. Of course, everyone was helping him in his cause.

"After lunch, how would you like to give Mark a little orientation of our offices and of some of the operations, Ron?" Andrew asked.

Ron broke out into a big grin. "It'll be a pleasure," he said.

In all honesty, Mark didn't have a clue that Ron was gay. The arousal in his groin was scaring him and he tried to put carnal thoughts of Ron out of his mind. He wasn't being too successful.

"I'm just going to show you around the office; orient you to our various enterprises and introduce you to people. I'll leave the bookkeeping orientation to Hank. He can do that on your first day," Ron explained.

After the orientation, Ron invited Mark to his office for a little chat. Mark was beside himself. If he didn't control his urges and his growing erection, this big guy might deck him. The first thing he saw when he went into Ron's office was a picture of two exceptionally handsome teen age boys on his desk. That cinched Mark's belief that Ron was straight arrow.

"I'm trying to convey a sense of family to you, Mark. Why do you look so nervous? Please relax. You won't find a pleasanter, more relaxed, work place than this one," Ron said. "Andrew and Freddie are too good to be true. They take care of their own."

Mark wondered what Ron meant by *they take care of their own.* Was something shady going on? He concluded that he merely meant, the office staff, and he tried to relax.

Ron decided to go right to the heart of his feelings. He had no idea that Mark did not know that he was gay. "Are you busy tonight? Do you have a date?" Ron asked.

Mark still didn't get it. He thought that Ron was just making friendly small talk. "No, I'm perfectly free tonight. I do have a tentative date for tomorrow night, but I'm not sure yet. Why did you ask me?"

"Frankly I'd like to have dinner with you. Sorry if I wasn't making myself clear."

"You want to have dinner with me?" Mark asked incredulously.

"Sure man. You're hot. I think you're better looking than your brother and he gets my juices going whenever I see him."

Mark broke out laughing. "Please don't hate me if I'm getting this all wrong, but are you gay?"

"Yes, Freddie told me that you were gay. Didn't they say anything about me?"

"I'm afraid not. I would love to have dinner with you tonight, and furthermore now I don't have to be afraid to stand up." Mark stood up and Ron could see that his trousers were tenting. They both broke out laughing.

Andrew, Kyle, Freddie and Scott decided to surprise Andrew's parents, and Sam and Jean, by flying down to Florida for the New Year. They worked it out so that Andrew knocked on his parent's door at the exact same moment that Freddie knocked on Sam's. Moments later, everybody was assembled at the Stanley's. After some discussion, Sam and Jean cancelled their plans to celebrate at a gay bar, and Dave and Anna gave up their plans to celebrate in the condo social hall. They decided that they would celebrate together in Sam and Jean's apartment. Anna and Jean volunteered to do all the shopping and the cooking.

Andrew and Kyle stayed with Andrew's parents. They put John up on the sleep sofa. David and Anna liked him immediately and oohed and aahed over the pictures of his family. Freddie and Scott stayed with Sam and Jean. Their bodyguards, Art and Ernie shared the third bedroom and everyone was invited to the party. Mel lucked out and got to spend the holiday at home. It was the most festive holiday any of them could ever remember. It was with great reluctance that the boys and their bodyguards returned to New York.

Ron and Mark celebrated the New Year by getting to know each other in Ron's bed for the first time. They were falling deeply in love.

Somehow the months flew by and Memorial Day weekend was staring them in the face. Ron approached Kyle and asked him if he would allow him to open the cabin and get it ready for the season before he and Andrew went down for the first time. He explained that he and Mark would like a week off for a honeymoon. Kyle got so excited he grabbed Ron in a bear hug. It was a case of bigger hugging big, and Ron thought his ribs would break.

After Ron and Mark cleared their vacation time at the office, Kyle gave Ron the key to the cabin, driving directions, and instructions for turning on all the utilities. Andrew took Ron aside and told him about the hidden butcher knives. He asked him to please not disturb the knives and to leave them in place. Ron did not question his boss. Every bodyguard knew the story of the Rodriguez cousins. It was a family secret, and if it ever got out, the informant would pay with his life. However, very few people were aware that Andrew still suffered paranoiac episodes as a result of the incident, and certainly nobody spoke of it. Kyle begged him to go for therapy, but he kept insisting that it was unnecessary. It became the only cause of dissension between them, but fortunately, their love was strong enough to surmount it.

Mark and Ron drove up to the cabin separately, in a car and a camper. Their intention was to leave the camper on the premises for the use of the bodyguards during the summer months. They themselves would use the bedroom in the cabin. They intended to spend the entire week in bed so they brought plenty of food with them.

They did everything on Kyle's list and stocked the cabin with all the food. When everything was done, and the cabin was habitable, they kissed each other passionately. This was going to be the first time they would be alone since they met, and they intended for it to be memorable, a real honeymoon. For his part, Ron was anxious to make up for years lost, and Mark was there to support him. Although they were both versatile, Ron preferred to be a top and Mark preferred to be a bottom. Once during the week, Ron was inside Mark's ass for almost two hours without a break. When finally Ron vacated Mark's sanctuary, Mark cried because he felt such a void.

When they did take a break, they would sit on the grass facing the lake. The temperature barely went above 55 degrees, but they sat naked, huddled together, covered by a blanket or two, as the cold lake breezes blew against their bodies. They should have been chilled to the bone, but they only felt the warmth of their bodies.

They would sit in silence for hours, staring at the lake, until one of them would whisper, "I love you so much." Then they would both jump up and head for the bed of their desires. They had heard often enough from Andrew and Kyle about how they had met here, and about their passionate first love encounter. Now Freddie and Scott also used the cabin as a romantic getaway place. Ron dubbed the cabin, "The Love Hotel" and decided to make a sign for Kyle to hang over the front door when he came down for the first time this coming season.

True to his word, Ron had the sign ready just before the Memorial Day weekend. Kyle, Andrew, Freddie and Scott, all drove up to the cabin on Friday evening for the big weekend. Kyle and Andrew would stay on for the week and Freddie and Scott would go home Monday evening and return again on Friday evening. The first thing they did on arrival was hang the sign over the front door. The bodyguards followed discreetly in another car and they quickly occupied the camper.

Sam and Jean had made so many friends in Florida, and the weather was so temperate in May, that they decided to stay until mid June, before driving home. The Stanley's always returned to New York at the end of June as well. Sam and Jean promised their friends that they would return no later than November 1.

Since Kyle and Andrew were staying for the week, they claimed the bedroom, and Freddie and Scott got their sleeping bags ready on the bedroom floor. The four of them had gotten to sleeping in the same room if they couldn't share a bed. It didn't bother either couple if one of them was engaged in passionate sex and the other couple wasn't. They knew that at some point in the weekend they would all enjoy each other.

Saturday morning Kyle and Scott drew the kitchen patrol. They were busy making breakfast while Andrew and Freddie sat out on the lawn facing the lake. Freddie had his arm around Andrew's shoulder and Andrew's head was lying on Freddie's arm.

"We are so lucky," Freddie said, "to have what we have, but most important, to have each other."

"I know," Andrew said with a cracking voice. "My life is so full of love. I'm always afraid that something will come along and spoil it."

"Nothing is going to spoil it," Freddie said emphatically. "Please Andrew, try to forget all those bad things and come back to us. You've got to stop jumping every time a door creeks. You are surrounded by bodyguards and so many people who love you. You have nothing to fear, I promise you."

"I know all that intellectually, but I can't seem to shake the fear."

"Will you go for therapy? Will you at least try? I know a great shrink. I went to him when I was old enough to realize the source of Uncle Sam's great wealth. Then again, I went to him when that Rodriguez ape told me that Sam had killed my parents. He really helped me cope with everything, and I think you should see him."

"Kyle's been bugging me too. If it's that obvious and that bad, I should see him, if not for myself, then for Kyle's sake."

"Atta boy," Freddie said. "I'll give you his name and his number." They were lying side by side. Freddie rolled over on top of Andrew. They began to kiss passionately and Freddie was squeezing Andrew's hard cock.

"I need to fuck you, Bro," Freddie said.

"Later," a stern voice interrupted them. It was Scott calling them to breakfast.

Andrew checked the slip of paper with Dr. Morgan's name and address. He was in one of the worst sections of Manhattan without a bodyguard. He had dismissed Ernie telling him that he had a very private errand to attend to. Now, looking around, he hoped that Ernie was around somewhere out of sight. The building in front of him was run down and looked condemned. But surely Freddie wouldn't have sent him here if he would be in danger.

He entered the building and found Suite 101. He opened the door into a reception room, but the room was empty, so he sat down in a chair. No sooner did he sit down when a door opened, and Dr. Morgan said, "Don't sit there come into my office."

Dr. Morgan had a bit of a strange accent and looked very much like Dracula without a cape. "Don't dawdle," he said. "I haven't got all day."

Andrew went into the doctor's office. He was not feeling too secure. The doctor sat him in a lounge chair and the doctor sat in a wing back chair facing him.

"How do you hope to benefit from seeing me?" the doctor asked.

"I hope to get over the fear that someone is going to spring out of nowhere and kill me."

"I doubt you have enough money for the cure," the doctor sniggered.

"Oh but I do. I'm quite wealthy, I assure you," Andrew started to plead.

The doctor suddenly began to laugh so loudly, that he had to put his hand to his side. As he did, his other hand miraculously held a big butcher knife. He started at Andrew. Suddenly four more brutes emerged from the walls. All were wielding butcher knives and coming at Andrew. He began to scream. He kept right on screaming even after his three bedroommates woke him up.

Andrew could feel Kyle's huge arms wrapped around him, comforting him, and he began to calm down. In time, he came to realize that it was just a nightmare and he was not in harm's way.

"We have to start curing you," Kyle said emphatically. "Come with me."

Andrew followed Kyle dutifully into the living room. "Now," Kyle said, "I want you to remove the butcher knives from between the sofa cushions and return them to the cutlery drawer in the kitchen."

Andrew turned pale. How did he know? Did Ron or Mark tell him? No, they would never do that. He had warned them on pain of death.

"How did you know?" Andrew asked sheepishly.

"One of them nearly pierced my thigh when I sat down on it yesterday. My God, Andy, they are more dangerous where they are than in a drawer. I could remove them, but I insist that you do it."

"I can't," Andrew said slightly whimpering.

"You must. It will be your first step toward recovery. If you don't, I swear, I'll sell the cabin and we'll never come here again."

"Please, Kyle, don't do that. You know how much this place means to me. I love it here," Andrew whined.

"Then just do it," Kyle insisted.

Andrew reached for the first knife. It felt like it weighed a ton, and he could hardly lift it. It took great effort, but he finally removed the first knife from under the cushion. He walked at a snail's pace to the kitchen and replaced the knife in the drawer. Reluctantly he repeated the process with the second knife. When he was finished, his body seemed to shrivel and Kyle had to support him.

"I'm proud of you," Kyle said.

"I didn't realize how heavy those knives were."

"Let's go back to sleep now, and we'll talk more about it in the morning." They went back to bed and Freddie and Scott cuddled into a single sleeping bag.

At last, Andrew did make an appointment with Dr. Morgan. His office was located on Fifth Avenue overlooking Central Park. It was one of Manhattan's poshest neighborhoods. The building was manned with security guards, and before they allowed Andrew to enter, they called the doctor's office to confirm his appointment. This was a far cry from Andrew's nightmare.

Andrew was taken into an office that looked like a sitting room at some hunting lodge. He relaxed immediately, and that was the purpose of the décor. Dr. Morgan came in a moment later. He was no more than 5' 5" tall, and a good thirty pounds overweight. His blue eyes twinkled, and his pudgy reddened cheeks were invitations to pinching. Andrew thought that in another twenty years if the good doctor grew a beard, he could pass for Santa Claus. In short, he liked him, and felt comfortable immediately.

After they introduced each other, Dr. Morgan asked Andrew to take his seat again. "Talk to me," he said.

During the course of therapy, Dr. Morgan was able to get Andrew to recall an incident in his early life. He and Andrew came to realize that this incident had always been a source of fear for Andrew and when he was twice kidnapped, his fears were exacerbated.

Andrew had just celebrated his fourteenth birthday and was in his first year of high school. He had accelerated in middle school and was six months to a year younger than his classmates. He had already begun to struggle with his sexual identity. He knew he was strong and brave enough to come out if he wanted to, but he wasn't sure yet so he kept his little secret.

He, and his best friend, Freddie Grant, were just leaving the school building to head on home, when they heard a commotion in the school yard. They went to investigate. Four big brutes were beating a thin, gaunt boy with their fists. Even though the boy was obviously unconscious, they kept on beating him.

"Here's what we do to faggots," one of them yelled. "We give them tickets to their trip to hell."

"Fucking faggot," the others yelled. One of them pulled a switchblade from his pocket and calmly started to cut the poor victim's face. Everyone was standing around doing nothing. Andrew was frozen in place, unable to move until Freddie yelled out, "The cops are on their way. Better scram, everyone." And everyone began to run away including the four brutes.

Freddie ran to the unfortunate victim. "Call for an ambulance," he yelled at Andrew, "and hurry." Andrew ran back into the school, and into the principal's office. The principal's secretary dialed 911, and ran out to help.

Freddie was trying to stop the bleeding on the boy's face with his handkerchief, but it wasn't doing much good. He removed his tee shirt and used that instead, applying as much pressure as he could. When the paramedics arrived, they told Freddie that his actions probably saved the boys life, but he would need a lot of surgery to restore his face to a semblance of humanity.

None of the witnesses could identify the maniacs who beat up the boy. They were older than high schoolers and certainly didn't attend the private school that Andrew and Freddie attended. They were never apprehended.

Dr. Morgan concluded that Andrew had lived his whole life in dread of being beaten and knifed because of his sexuality. This fear was deeply buried in his subconscious. The first invasion by Carl and Joey Barkin had opened the door slightly and the second invasion by the Rodriguez cousins had blown the door fully open.

When Andrew realized that his fears did not originate from his two kidnapping incidents, but stemmed from fears of being beaten cruelly because of his sexual orientation, he began to heal. He was no longer frightened by the fact that he was gay. That had been a childhood fear. It took several more sessions with Dr. Morgan, but little by little the seven veils of fear were dropped and Andrew's nightmares stopped.

He looked forward to the upcoming Labor Day weekend. He, Kyle, Freddie and Scott were going to The Love Hotel, and before they left, they would be closing up the cabin. Andrew's parents had decided to live year round in Boca Raton and they had moved out of their apartment during the summer. They would not be spending the two weeks after Labor Day at the cabin this year.

Sam and Jean also decided to spend most of their time in Florida. They announced that as long as they were able, they would travel during the hot summer months, and spend the rest of the year in Boca. Freddie put twin beds in Sam's room for the two bodyguards remaining in the house. The house was less crowded, less noisy and much more relaxed since Sam and Jean decided to become full time Florida residents.

Sam and Jean talked Mel and his wife into moving down to Florida. They said jokingly that all good grandparents did that so their kids would have a place to vacation in the winter. Sam and Jean bought them a beautiful condo nearby to theirs, and Mel became their permanent body guard.

When Ron opened the twelfth retail shop, he needed an assistant, so he hired Mark's brother John. Ernie and Art then became full time bodyguards to the residents of The Town House. The four brothers were together most of the time and so one or the other of the bodyguards was now able to spend more time with his family, and that pleased everyone.

They even began to alternate weekends at The Love Hotel. They became so much a part of the family, that their presence was hardly noticeable and certainly never an intrusion. On warm summer evenings, when the brothers went skinny dipping in the lake, the bodyguard on duty would often join them. There was no longer any embarrassment about being part of a gay naked group. The bodyguards just took it in stride, even when their charges grabbed at each other.

The cabin at the inlet became a peaceful getaway haven for the family. In the winter they flew down to Florida whenever they could get away. They stayed with Andrew's parents or with Sam and Jean. When at home in The City, they went to sporting events, theater, opera, ballet and museums together. They four of them often had dinner at their favorite gay bars and restaurants. At home, they made love together.

The further in time that they removed themselves from Sam's old business ventures, the more they obtained anonymity, and the more secure they became. In time, they found jobs for Ernie and Art in their legitimate enterprises, and stopped using bodyguards altogether. Sam and Jean objected, but their objections fell on deaf ears.

One warm summer day in the middle of the week, Kyle and Andrew were alone together at the cabin. They never bothered to wear clothes and were a little shocked when there was a knock on the door. They both grabbed robes and Kyle went to answer the door.

"I'm really sorry to disturb you," a handsome young man said. "I was rowing on the lake and my strength just gave out. I'm moored at your dock in the inlet and I wonder if I could get something to drink, and rest up before I return to The Waterfall Lodge."

"Sure, come on in," Kyle said. "Would you like a beer or something softer?"

"Ice water would do just fine," the young man said. He put out his hand. "My name is Marty Soren. I'm staying at the lodge for a few days. I start teaching math at SUNY Albany in a couple of weeks. It's my first gig."

Kyle shook his hand. "I'm Kyle Farrell," he said. "I bought this place as a hideaway when I taught English Lit at Albany. I teach at CCNY now. And this good looking guy is my partner, Andrew Stanley." Andrew was still amazed at how easily Kyle could let people know that he was gay, and he was still so reticent.

"Your partner?" Marty reiterated. He broke out into a big grin.

"Have a seat," Kyle said, motioning toward the kitchen table. "I'll pour the ice water."

Kyle and Andrew sat down at the table with the young man.

"This is so déjà vu," Andrew said.

"What do you mean?" Marty asked. Andrew told Marty the story of how he and Kyle met and fell in love.

"If you had come through the front door instead of the back, you would have seen the sign over the front door, The Love Hotel. That's what one of our friends named the place and he had the sign made for us."

'What a great story," Marty said. "I'm jealous. I'm still looking for the right girl for me."

"Well, maybe some of the magic will rub off," Kyle said.

"We were just going for a swim in the lake," Andrew said. "If you want to, you can join us. If not, just rest up, and you can leave whenever you feel you've got your strength back.

Marty was about to accept their offer to join in the swim, but they both removed their robes. Marty expected to see swim suits. He was a bit perturbed to see that they were naked.

"I think I'll head back to the lodge," he said. "There's a young lady staying there that has my interest. I've asked her to have dinner with me tonight. Maybe the magic *will* rub off. We shall see." He tried hard not to look at the two naked men's private area. It was a struggle.

"Good," Andrew said. We're having dinner at the lodge tonight. We'll look for you. Just close the door when you leave." He and Kyle walked out together. Marty saw Kyle take Andrew's hand as they walked toward the lake. He was a bit envious. He finished his drink and placed the glass in the sink. He walked toward the dock and untied his canoe. He got back in, and rowed toward the lodge.

As he pulled away, he glanced back and could see Andrew and Kyle standing knee deep in the water. He could make out their erect cocks rubbing against their bodies. Kyle was much taller than Andrew, which prevented their cocks from rubbing together. They had their arms wrapped around each other and they were kissing passionately. Marty didn't bother to wave to them as he pulled away. They wouldn't have noticed him.

"Make a wish," Marty thought he heard a voice say. "This is a magic place."

"I wish someday to find someone who will love me like those two guys love each other," he prayed, and continued to row back to the lodge with a big grin on his face.

CHAPTER ELEVEN

Andrew and Kyle arrived at Waterfall Lodge long before their dinner reservation hour. They wanted to be sure to see James Harper before he left for the day. James was delighted to see them and gave them each a bear hug.

"It's always great to see you two," he said. "It always reminds me that there is an outside world."

"And for us," Kyle remarked, "seeing you reminds us of our secluded little getaway cabin."

"I'm not sure how much longer The Waterfall Lodge will remain open. I suspect that it might shut down after Labor Day," James said, quite remorsefully. "The owners have it up for sale. It's been on the market for almost a year and they haven't had a single offer yet. If nothing comes through by Labor Day, they're shutting down. It's not that the place isn't doing well, but they are getting on and just want to retire."

Strange as it seems, Andrew and Kyle had only met the owners on rare occasions. They were a couple in their late seventies, and Mr. Powell was confined to a wheel chair from wounds suffered during the Korean War.

Andrew's head began to swim with an idea. He excused himself, went into a private space, and called Freddie.

"What would you think about buying The Waterfall Lodge?" he asked. "It might not be much of a money maker, but think of what a haven it would be for us and our families. The cabin is great, but it's uncomfortable when we come out here together. This way we could escape year round and have every amenity. Sharon and Mike could even vacation here with their families, not to mention Sam and Jean and all our parents. It would be so wonderful."

"How do you know it's for sale?" Freddie asked.

"James just told us. It's been on the market for nearly a year without a bite. I'll bet we could get a real bargain."

"OK Bro, go do your thing. Get us a good price, but don't even think of screwing those nice people."

"I got you babe. I'll see to it."

He returned to where James and Kyle were chatting. "How can I get in touch with the Powells?" Andrew asked. "Gardini Enterprises is interested in purchasing this place."

Kyle's jaw dropped open and then he broke out into a big grin.

"Don't worry Kyle. We can still use the cabin in the summer, but we'll be able to come out here all the rest of the year."

"We'd better buy a good set of snow tires," Kyle said while tapping his forehead with his index finger, as if to say, *See, I think of everything.*

"Mr. and Mrs. Powell will be here tomorrow morning. I'll call and alert them," James advised Andrew. Why don't you come for breakfast tomorrow morning and you can meet them and discuss business."

James was about to leave, but Andrew took him by the arm to stop him. "If I buy the place, James, will you manage it for me and Freddie?"

"Work for you?" James asked. "It would be my pleasure. My partner, Richard, is retiring at the end of the year. He could help me, and I wouldn't have to worry about his having nothing to do. Plus, I wouldn't have to worry about finding a job in my late fifties. Thanks for the offer, Andrew."

"I feel better already knowing that I can depend on you," Andrew said. He shook James' hand and said, "I'll see you in the morning then."

It was still early for dinner so Kyle and Andrew decided to take a stroll down by the lake. This time they were not alone. They spotted Marty sitting on a bench facing the lake. A young woman was sitting quite close to him. They couldn't see her face, but they could tell that she was quite slim. *Marty is very good looking,* Kyle thought. *I'll bet she's beautiful.*

They approached Marty and greeted him. He jumped up and pumped both their hands. Then he remembered his manners. He introduced them to Laurie Payne. She was absolutely stunning, and Marty informed her, "These two guys just about saved my life this afternoon."

"Well then, I must thank you also," Laurie said. "If you hadn't been so gallant, I'd be sitting here alone tonight." She smiled at Marty.

"Kyle used to teach at Albany also, Laurie," Marty informed her. "Maybe you can give me some advice, Kyle," He looked toward Kyle.

"Anything goes," Kyle said. "There is only one rule that all the good teachers adhere to, and that is to never get involved with a student."

Marty groaned. "Laurie will be a senior there this coming semester."

Kyle saved the day. "The rule doesn't count," he said, "if you are already involved. Are you?"

The two young people looked at each other and smiled shyly.

"In that case," Andrew said, "we'll go in to dinner and leave you two alone. It was very nice meeting you Laurie."

When Kyle and Andrew left, Marty said, "They are a gay couple you know. I have never seen such love between two people. When I left their cabin, I silently prayed that I could find someone who would love me like they love each other."

Laurie looked deep into Marty's eyes. She pulled his head down and kissed him passionately.

Gardini Enterprises and Mr. and Mrs. Powell arrived at a selling price which was less than the Powells had hoped for. But based on the depressed economy and the net profits of the lodge, both parties were satisfied. The Powells were happy in the knowledge that their retirement was assured. Gardini Enterprises put down forty percent of the purchase price and had no trouble securing a mortgage for the balance at a local community bank. The sale became effective on September 30.

The first reservations that James took for Gardini Enterprises were from Dr. and Mrs. Stanley, who booked the last two weeks of August for the following summer. Shortly thereafter, Jean Gay booked two rooms, one for him and Sam Gardini and one for Mel Thomas and his wife for all of July and August. Mel remained Sam's bodyguard, but nobody was fooled. Mel had become like the old family retainer in a Merchant Ivory film. Sharon booked two rooms for the last two weeks in August when her parents would be there, and Mike booked the same two weeks for his family. They all booked at greatly discounted prices, and Freddie said jokingly that it better be a good season for lovers and other strangers.

In the meantime, the lodge was booked solid for the winter months. It snowed steadily that year, and the skiers came up in droves. James was pleased to report healthy profits at the end of every week. Richard worked a deal to retire a month earlier, because James really needed his help. The only slack period they had was late spring and James and Richard needed the break for their own vacation.

Kyle and Andrew, Scott and Freddie worked it out so that they all spent both Thanksgiving and Christmas in Boca Raton. They were only gone for a couple of work days and no school days. Freddie and Andrew had no reticence about leaving the office in the capable hands of Hank and Mark, ably assisted by Ron.

Now that they were owners, Andrew and Freddie stayed at the lodge every other weekend with their spouses. To their credit, they acted like good hoteliers. They mingled with the guests, and even asked the New Yorkers to call them in The City for dinner out together or just to say hello.

Every few weekends, Marty and Laurie Soren came for a weekend. They had been married during the first week of November. Marty told Kyle that this way he didn't have to break the rule about fraternizing with the student body, since they were previously involved.

"I'm really happy," Marty told Kyle. "I love teaching, and I love the lady I come home to. I'm a lucky guy."

"Yes," Kyle said. "I can see that."

The guest population was also filled with friends of the Gardini family. Some were mutual friends, some were friends from CCNY, some were business associates, but whatever the source, they booked a stay at the lodge and they all loved the rustic atmosphere. Sometime in early May, James told them that the lodge was booked solid from June through September. It was developing that their investment was a good one, both financially and socially.

Only one thing marred their serenity. About once a week in the summer, and whenever possible the rest of the year, Andrew and Kyle drove to the gorge where the Barkins and Rodriguezes lay buried. They peered into the deep waters below. The waterfall kept the waters churning at this point and the lake was so deep that it was impossible to see below the surface. Still, they felt better when they could determine that there was no sign of the evidence, and that it was forever buried.

There was nobody alive to seek out the Rodriguez cousins. As for the Barkin twins, Mary Barkin never knew who her sons worked for, and when they disappeared, she didn't know where to begin to look for them. Eventually she faced the fact that they were not returning. She naturally assumed that they were living incognito in some remote city, hiding out from something or someone, too afraid to even contact her. She stopped looking for them and stopped inquiring about them, believing that it was for their own safety. In short, nobody missed the four bodies lying buried in the deep.

One early October day, Andrew's secretary buzzed him. "Ron Harte is here to see you, Andrew," she said. "He doesn't have an appointment."

What the hell is she talking about? Since when does Ron need an appointment? He usually barges right in. There was a knock on the door and Andrew yelled, "Come on in."

Imagine his surprise when he saw a young man, no older than eighteen years old enter the room. He looked exactly as Ron might have looked about twenty years ago. Andrew stood and held out his hand, which the young man shook.

"You have to be Ron's son," he said. You look just like him."

"Everybody says so, but I'm an inch shorter," Ron, Jr. said.

"Did you come to see your father? I'm afraid he's out of town on business. He won't be back until Friday night and he won't be back in the office until Monday," Andrew informed the young man.

"Actually, I came to see you. I'm a freshman at CCNY. My English Lit teacher is Dr. Farrell. I got to talking with him one day, and told him that I was majoring in accounting, and would love to get a part time job in some accounting office. He suggested I go see you. At first I was hesitant, because I know my dad works for you, but then I figured maybe that would help me, rather than hurt me."

Andrew grew a little suspicious. "Can you tell me how you came to be talking to Dr. Farrell so intimately?"

"Oh sure, Mr. Stanley. Dr. Farrell is very open about his being gay. He often mentions you in his lectures and how much you two guys love each other."

"He does?" Andrew asked, pleased but incredulous.

"Uh huh! Anyway, I have reason to believe…. I think I might be…."

"Gay!" Andrew finished the sentence. Ron Jr. nodded.

"I don't know if you know, but Dr. Farrell is always encouraging his students to consult him with any of their problems. He has a reputation of being the best teacher and the most compassionate on campus. I needed to talk to someone about my, er, situation. I can't talk to my step dad. We aren't that close. My kid brother and he are close, but I'm not. I'm afraid to talk to my real dad. You know he's a big, macho guy, and I'm afraid he would be disappointed in me if he knew."

Andrew couldn't believe it. Nobody had ever told Ron's son that Ron was gay. He figured that it would be up to Ron to do the honors. He certainly wasn't going to.

"Was Dr. Farrell able to help you with your *situation*?"

"Yes, he gave me some good advice. Basically, he told me not to worry so much about it, and to just let things unfold in their natural order. He was also positive that my dad would take the news better than I expected, but I really doubt that."

"Have you got a boyfriend?" Andrew asked out of curiosity.

"God no!" Ron stated emphatically. "I don't know where I stand yet myself." He looked down at the floor. "But I sure would like to find out."

A voice from Andrew's deep past said to Ron, "It'll happen."

"Why don't you sit here and wait for me, son. I want to go to accounting and discuss what we might have for you."

"Thank you sir."

Andrew literally ran to the accounting office. Hank and Ron were on the same business trip. Mark and several clerks were holding down the fort. Andrew grabbed Mark and pulled him into Hank's private office.

"What's going on?" Mark asked thoroughly alarmed. Andrew filled him in on everything that had happened up to this moment.

"He has no clue that his father is gay, and certainly would not suspect that you are his father's lover. Don't spill the beans. I suggest you leave that for Ron. I wonder if Ron knows that his son is gay."

"I doubt that very much. He would have discussed it with me. Don't worry; my lips are sealed. I won't tell either one of them about the other," Mark said.

"I'll bring him to see you. Give him that part time job even if you don't need him, and we'll let the chips fall where they may." Andrew buzzed his secretary from Hank's phone and asked her to bring Ron Jr. around. When Ron came into the office he read the sign on the door which said, Henry Morrissey, CFO. He reached out his hand and before Andrew could make introductions Ron said, "Hello Mr. Morrissey. I'm Ron Harte, Jr. It's a pleasure to meet you."

Both Andrew and Mark laughed.

"No son," Andrew said. Hank's on the same business trip with your dad. This is Mark Davis, Hank's assistant."

Ron blushed, "I'm so sorry Mr. Davis."

"It's quite alright son. Don't let it bother you. I just can't get over how much you look like your dad."

When Ron threw open the apartment door Friday evening after returning from Los Angeles, he fell directly into Mark's arms devouring him with kisses. "It's hell going on a business trip with a straight guy," he said, trying to tease Mark. The only reaction he got was a shit eaten grin.

"I can see that you are bursting to give me some news," Ron said. "Spill it!"

"I hired a new part time accounting clerk a couple of days ago."

"So why the look?" Ron needed to know. "That's hardly big news."

"It is if you consider that he's related to you."

Ron's jaw dropped. He grew silent and looked thoroughly deflated. "My son?" he asked. Mark nodded.

"This is awkward. He doesn't know that I'm gay."

"I know. Andrew told me," Mark said.

"How would Andrew know?"

"I don't know. I didn't ask him."

"Well, he's eighteen. He was bound to find out sooner or later. At least I know that Rhonda kept her word not to tell the boys."

"Will you tell him?" Mark asked. "It's no secret in the office. It might come out, and I want to love him too."

"Yes, it's time he knew the truth. But I must make it clear to him that my being gay had nothing to do with my divorce. Rhonda dumped me before she knew."

"I know you'll handle it well," Mark said. "I'll be there if you need me."

Ron returned to the office on Monday morning. In order to accommodate his son's class schedule, Ronnie's hours were from one to five every Monday, Tuesday and Friday. Poor Ron fidgeted all morning. He couldn't concentrate on his work.

His son arrived at 12:45 and went right to accounting. As soon as he could, Mark alerted Ron that his son was in the office. Ron ran over to the accounting office. As soon as he spotted his son, he embraced him. Ronnie hugged back.

"Weren't you going to stop at my office and say hello, Ronnie?" Ron asked.

"Sure dad, but I wanted to do it after working hours. I really need to talk to you about a few things."

"That's great. Come by at five. We'll have dinner together and we can talk. I need to talk to you about a lot of stuff also."

While Mark was giving Ronnie work to do and explaining the process to him, he inadvertently was very touchy feely. He wasn't even aware of it. Ronnie was so much like his father that Mark was merely reacting to natural instinct. For his part, Ronnie was enjoying the intimacy with another male. He had no idea the other male was his father's lover.

For Ronnie, the afternoon went much too fast. He really enjoyed the work and the friendliness of his co-workers. For Ron, the afternoon extended into eternity. At last there was a knock on the door.

"Come in and leave the door open," the father said. He knew so little about his own son that he had to ask, "What kind of food would you like tonight son? Italian? Chinese?"

"Chinese would be great Dad,"

"Good, we'll go to my favorite restaurant in Chinatown."

Mark poked his head in. "Good night, Rons," he said. "I'll see you both tomorrow." Ronnie was certain that he saw Mark wink at his father, but then again, he could have been wrong.

Ron grabbed his coat and put his arm around his son as he escorted him to the elevator. Downstairs they grabbed a cab and Ron gave the cabbie instructions. As soon as they were settled in the cab, Ron asked, "What did you want to talk to me about, son?"

"I'd rather wait until we're in the restaurant, Dad. Let's try to get a quiet table away from other people. OK?"

"Sounds serious, son."

"Maybe, maybe not."

The waiter served them both wonton soup. Ron didn't want to pressure Ronnie so they ate in silence. When Ronnie had his fill, he pushed his plate aside and looked at his father. *This is it,* Ron thought and prepared himself for the worst.

"Dad, I have something to tell you." He hesitated.

"Go ahead son. You can tell me anything. When you love someone you should be able to tell him anything or it isn't really love."

Ronnie nodded and continued. "Did you know that Mr. Stanley is gay?"

"Yes, I knew. But…"

"His partner, Dr. Farrell, is my English Lit professor, and he's the one who told me to see Mr. Stanley about getting a part time job. He encouraged it even after I told him that you worked for Mr. Stanley."

"I'm glad you didn't let that stop you, Ronnie."

"Dad, Dr. Farrell is very openly gay. That's why I went to see him. I needed someone I could talk to. When I told him that I was gay, he advised me strongly to tell you and mom."

Ron was dumbfounded, speechless, and unable to react. He sat like a statue and Ronnie began to shake. "Do you hate me, Dad?" Ronnie began to weep.

"Good god. I don't hate you. I love you. I love you more than ever." Ron jumped up and embraced his son who was weeping into his father's shoulder." Just then, the waiter came to the table with their entrees. The two men grew silent until he left.

"You said that you had things to tell me also, Dad. I think it's time to put all our dirty laundry on the table," Ronnie said, anticipating some juicy stuff from dad.

"The first thing that you must know is that my divorce was all my doing. Your mom was blameless. I was just never home. Certainly I was never there for her. I made better than average wages, and you were all well provided for but I realize now that it wasn't enough. I want to apologize to you and your brother, right here and right now, for not being a father to you. It's ironic. Now that I have time for visitation, your brother doesn't want to see me. Perhaps you can intercede for me.

"That having been said, something happened to me after your mother and I split. As you know now all my employers are gay. Somewhere along the line, I realized that I was beginning to be attracted to men, especially to my employers. I was struck dumb. More and more I wanted to act on my desires. Finally, I confided in Freddie Grant, and his partner, Scott, who is also a professor at CCNY. Shall we say, they experimented with me, and helped me realize that I preferred to be with men more than with women.

"Andrew and Freddie introduced me to someone and I fell in love. I'm happy to tell you Ronnie that your old man is in a happy and monogamous relationship. We live in our old apartment and there is always room for you and your brother should you care to visit. Would you like to come home with me after dinner and meet him? I'll put you in a cab and send you home afterwards. I don't intend for you to use the subway this hour of the day."

Ronnie sat with his jaw hanging open. He was literally speechless.

"Please say something, Ronnie. Even if you want to disown me as a father, just say something to me. I'll go crazy if you don't. I can't tell you how much I need for you to accept me as a father and to accept my lifestyle. Even more importantly, I want you to meet my partner, and see why I love him so much."

"Are you really gay, Dad?" was all Ronnie could spit out.

Ron nodded his head. He was sobbing silently. Tears were smearing down his face. This time Ronnie stood up and embraced his father. "I love you, Dad, and I can't wait to meet your partner. Can we leave now?"

"Of course we can. Just let me call him and let him know that we are coming over."

"I'd love to stay at your place tonight, Dad, but I have no clothes for the morning or even a tooth brush. Could we spend the weekend together? I'd really like that and maybe I can convince Tommy to join us. I'm not sure how he'll take it when he finds out we're both gay. Does mom know?

"Yes, I told her soon after our divorce, but she said that it was up to me to tell you boys when you were ready. She's a smart lady, your mom. I am truly happy that she has found happiness."

In the cab going to Ron's apartment, Ron was giggling inside at the thought of Ronnie finding out that his immediate superior was his stepfather. *This will either be a hoot or a disaster,* Ron thought. He had butterflies in his stomach.

When Ron put his key in the door, it was Ronnie who had the butterflies. Most straight guys grew up wanting to have the kind of sex their fathers were having. Most gay boys didn't feel that way, of course. Ronnie knew that he used to be an exception, and so he found it very thrilling to be in the same boat now, wishing to have sex like his father. He couldn't wait to see the guy who his dad was fucking and maybe being fucked by.

They walked into the apartment and Mark Baker was standing and waiting for them. "Hi Ronnie," he said, and held out his arms letting Ronnie know that he wanted to embrace him.

Ronnie fell into Mark's arms and allowed himself to be hugged. After a while Mark released him and Ronnie started to giggle. "You're very lucky, Dad. When I met Mark the other day, I got the hots for him."

"Well, I am flattered," Mark said.

"Are we still alright at work?" Ronnie asked Mark, with real concern.

"Of course, we are."

Ronnie changed after that. He became open to his sexuality and came out to his mother and his stepfather. Neither was happy about it, but they accepted it. "Given the circumstances," he told them, "I would like to move in with dad. I'll come home as often as I can," he promised.

They were less than pleased to see him go, but Ronnie was eighteen, and Ron was paying his college expenses, so they had to submit to his wishes.

He was unable to get his kid brother, Tommy, to come and reconcile with his dad, but he vowed to keep trying.

In time, Ronnie met the entire 'family', and he became the son they never had nor would ever have. He had no idea, but Sam set up a very healthy trust fund for him, and he would someday be an extremely wealthy man. Everyone else treated him as if they had spawned him from their own loins. To his credit, Ronnie was fully aware of how blessed he was.

He began to have occasional sex with men he met at college, but the real love, which surrounded him in his new family life, eluded him. He kept thinking of Andrew's words, "It'll happen." *When?* He kept asking himself.

In his senior year, he was studying International Finance. The class was very small. The minimum number of students a class needed to have in order not to be scrubbed, was twelve. There were fourteen students in the class, all men. The professor was getting ready for retirement and there was even some doubt that International Finance would be taught the following year. While most of the class struggled with the course material, Ronnie and another student, Leo Jennetti, were shining aces. Professor Thompson was thrilled at how astute the two men were. He was of British origin and he began to invite them to his home for high tea and scones, and to discuss international finance together. He found the boys intellectually stimulating, and delighted in playing devil's advocate with them.

Understandably, Ronnie and Leo became good friends. One day as they were leaving Professor Thompson's home, Leo asked Ronnie if he would like to double date with him one Saturday night. Ronnie had been mentored by so many gay men, he didn't hesitate to tell Leo right out, "I'd love to go out on a double date with you, Leo, but I have two problems."

Leo looked unhappy. "It isn't me?" he asked concerned.

"That's 'I' Ron Corrected, "and no it isn't you. It's I. First of all, I am not seeing anyone right now and I have nobody to ask out, and second of all, I'm gay, flamingly so! If I had a date, he'd be a guy."

"Thank God! Thank God!" Leo said, looking heavenward.

"What?"

"Please don't let me frighten you away. We can talk about it if you get scared, but I'm gay also and I am so hot for you, it hurts. I can't believe that someone as good looking as you is unattached."

"That might be because until a second ago, I never met anyone who turned me on enough to spark an interest. Oh Leo, please let's go someplace where we can be alone and talk about this before I burst."

Ronnie took Leo to his dad's apartment where he had been living for almost three years. On the way, he explained his living situation with his two dads here, and the other dad living downtown with his mother.

All Leo could say was, "And I was afraid to come out to you. What a jerk."

Ronnie knew that Ron and Mark would not be home for at least another hour. He and Leo went into his room, and closed the door. They had intended to talk only and express their feelings for each other, but the minute the door closed, they were all over each other. They stripped so fast that they may possibly have set some sort of record. Without preliminaries, they were hard as rocks.

They knew they didn't have much time, so they threw themselves on Ronnie's bed, twisted into a 69 position and began to give each other life's most intimate pleasure. They both came so fast, it must have set another new record. They didn't hesitate to swallow each other's cum. Best of all, they both knew immediately that this was only the beginning of greater things to come.

While they were dressing, Ronnie asked, "Do your folks know?"

"I have never come out to them, but I've been told that parents seem to sense these things. Now I have reason to tell them. Will you be with me, when I do?"

"Of course, if it will make it easier for you."

When Ron and Mark came home, they found Leo and Ronnie sitting on the sofa, wrapped up together and kissing passionately. The two young men never even heard Ron and Mark enter the apartment.

"Ahem," Mark said. Ron just smiled. Ronnie and Leo jumped up from the sofa. Both of them were very red faced.

"Introduce us to your friend, Ronnie, and then if you want to continue, just carry on," Ron joked.

"Dad, Mark," Ronnie said. "I'd like you to meet someone very dear to me."

When Ronnie and Leo graduated, Ron and Mark made a big party at The Four Seasons. It was to be a double celebration. Of course, there was the graduation to celebrate, but the boys were also celebrating their commitment to be together. Sam, Jean and the Stanleys came in from Florida. Leo's parents, John, Hank, Andrew, Kyle, Freddie, Scott, and their siblings with their families were on the guest list.

Ron thought about it a very long time and in the end, he invited Rhonda, her husband and his son, Tommy. He was really shocked when they accepted the invitation. They already knew Leo, but they had never met Mark.

By now Tommy was getting ready to enter college. Kyle and Scott were delighted to hear that he was going to Buffalo, and the three of them spoke at length about the school and the city. Ron went out of his way to compliment Rhonda on the great job she had done with both boys.

Tommy was a young man now and very mature. Ron was afraid to speak to him alone, but Tommy came up to him. He was taller than both his father and his brother.

"I want to thank you dad for providing for me all these years and paying for my college education. I realize that you don't have to do that now that I'm eighteen."

Ron grabbed him in a bear hug. Tommy didn't resist. "I love you, son," Ron said sobbing. "I'm sorry if I hurt you."

"You didn't hurt me, Dad. I have a good life. I like Mark. I'm happy for you. When I met Leo, I realized that if I didn't accept him as part of my family and let him into my life, I would lose my brother. Then I realized that I had lost you for that very reason. I'd like to make up for it and be your son again."

Words failed Ron so he just kept hugging his son and crying. Mark watched from a distance and he cried too.

Kyle took Ronnie and Leo aside. He handed them the keys to the cabin on the inlet, and written instructions how to get there. "I want you two guys to use the cabin this weekend and next week. Andrew, Freddie, Scott, and I will be at The Waterfall Lodge over the weekend. It's across the lake from the cabin. Feel free to come over and join us for dinner.

"But be warned," Kyle said in a hushed voice. "The cabin is magical. It will cause strangers to fall in love, and lovers to fall more deeply in love. Do you think that you can handle that? It's where your father and Mark honeymooned, and look at them. Look at Andrew and me and look at Freddie and Scott. Every time we go to the cabin, our loves deepen. Don't question my sanity. You'll see. It'll happen."

It'll happen! That's what Andrew had said, Ronnie thought. *At the time, I thought he meant sex, but he meant love.*

"I can't wait to get there, Uncle Kyle," (It had been ages since Ronnie had called Kyle and Scott *professor.)*

"Me either," Leo echoed.

The next morning, they loaded the car and headed for the magic cabin.

ABOUT THE AUTHOR

Hank Brooks was born in Brooklyn, NY and lived most of his adult life in and around the New York City area.

He is very active in SAGE, a senior advocacy group for gay men and women.

He has three children and five grandsons. He is a retired CPA, and now lives with his partner, Leo, in Coconut Creek, Florida.

A Family Affair

and Other Erotic Gay Tales by

Hank Brooks

BROOKS

A FAMILY AFFAIR

A
Boner
Book

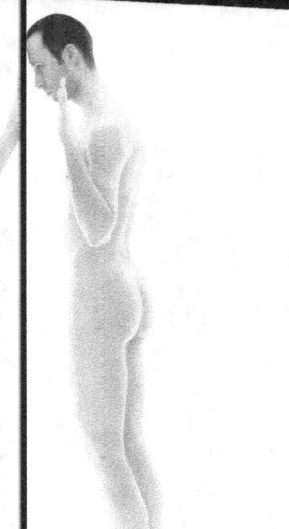

Impossible Love

a novel by

Hank Brooks

A
Boner
Book

Brooks

Impossible Love

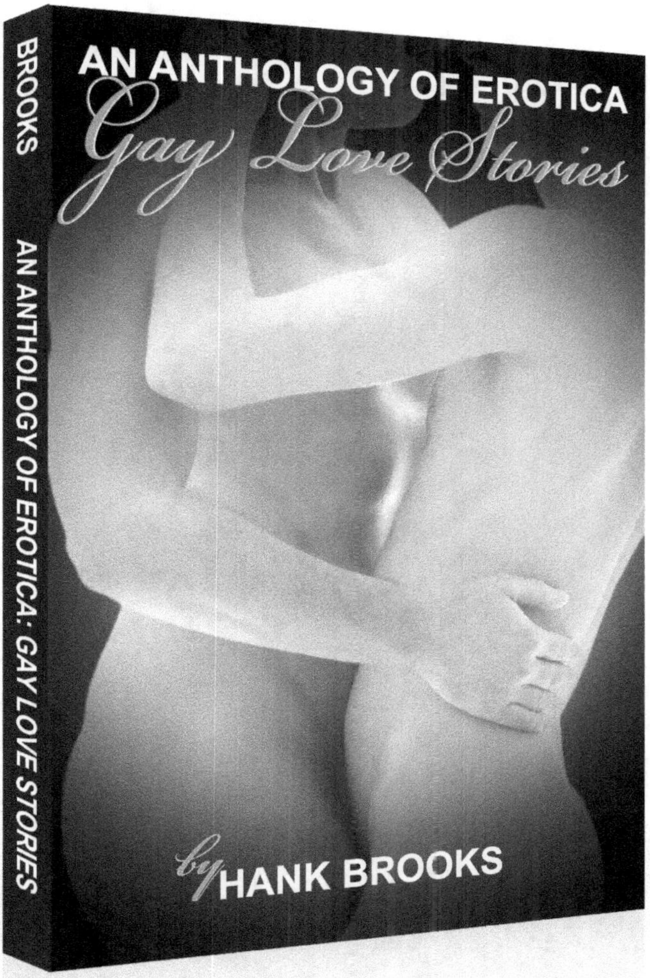
BROOKS
AN ANTHOLOGY OF EROTICA: GAY LOVE STORIES
AN ANTHOLOGY OF EROTICA
Gay Love Stories
by HANK BROOKS